USA TODAY BESTSELLING AUTHOR

RITA HERRON

SAFE WITH HIM

MANHUNT 3 SERIES

Beachside Reads
Norcross, GA 30092

Cover Design: Jeffery Olsen
Cover Photo: The Illustrated Romance, https://illustratedromance.com
Print Design: Dayna Linton, Day Agency
eBook Interior Design: Dayna Linton, Day Agency

ISBN: 978-1-949178-04-3 (Paperbook)
ISBN: 978-1-949178-05-0 (eBook)

Third Edition: 2018

10 9 8 7 6 5 4 3

Printed in the USA

To friend and fellow writer

Jennifer St. Giles for always plotting murder with me!

SAFE WITH HIM

PROLOGUE

"**K**AYLIE, SOMEONE'S IN THE house."

Kaylie Whittaker snapped her eyes open at her husband's husky whisper, the darkness nearly blinding her.

Joe gripped her hand. "I'm going to check it out. Go into CeCe's room and lock the door."

Fear shot through Kaylie. Their five-year-old daughter was sound asleep across the hall. Joe was right. She had to get to CeCe. If someone had broken in, she had to protect her.

Joe slid from bed, unlocked the drawer of his nightstand, and removed his .38. Kaylie took a deep breath, pushed the covers aside and reached for her cell phone to call 911.

But she'd left the phone downstairs.

Joe's gun flashed silver in the dark as he loaded it and tiptoed toward the door.

A noise downstairs made them both freeze. Footsteps. The wood floor squeaked.

Joe eased open their bedroom door, and Kaylie slid into the hallway past him, then darted across the hall to her daughter's room. She inched inside and crossed the room, padding quietly on the carpet.

She heard Joe starting down the steps, and she lowered herself onto the bed beside CeCe, not wanting to startle her, but knowing she had to hurry.

"Honey, wake up," she whispered as she gently shook CeCe. "We have to hide."

CeCe mumbled something in her sleep, and Kaylie lifted her from bed and cradled her against her. They couldn't crawl out the window; they were on the second floor.

It sounded as if the intruder had entered through the front door.

If she could reach the back staircase leading from the bonus room to the kitchen, she could sneak Kaylie outside through the back. Then she could run to the next-door neighbor's house and call for help.

Her chest tight with fear, she opened the door a fraction of an inch, but suddenly a man shoved it open and pushed her husband inside the room.

The man wore a dark mask, and black clothes and held a gun to Joe's temple.

A scream caught in Kaylie's throat.

"Get down on your knees," the man ordered her husband.

Joe looked at her with panicked eyes. "Kaylie . . ."

"Do it." The man pushed Joe to the floor. CeCe stirred, her eyes widening in terror.

"If you want money, there's cash in the safe," Joe said. "Take it. Take my car, whatever. Just don't hurt my family."

CeCe clutched at Kaylie's neck, her tiny body vibrating with fear.

"I have jewelry," Kaylie said. "You can have it all."

"Shut up." His crooked teeth gleamed in the faint light spilling through the window as he aimed the gun at Joe. "I want you to watch your family die."

Joe's gaze flew to hers, shock and fear glittering in his brown eyes.

"On your knees, lady."

"Please, she's just a little girl," Kaylie begged. "Don't hurt her."

The man's hand dug into Kaylie's shoulder with such force she winced and fell to her knees, clutching CeCe to her and trying to shield her.

With a menacing growl, the intruder turned his gun toward her.

Joe suddenly lunged up from the floor and rammed his body into the man. "Run, Kaylie, save CeCe."

A shot fired. Blood splattered onto the carpet.

Adrenaline surged through Kaylie, and she jumped up, raced into the hall and flew down the steps. CeCe clung to her, tears soaking Kaylie's pajama top as she ran toward the front door.

Behind her, another gunshot blasted the air. The sound of a man's grunt, then falling.

A second later, footsteps pounded behind her.

Oh, God, Joe was shot, and the man was coming after her.

She had to escape.

She threw open the door and darted to the right toward the neighbor's house. When she and Joe had chosen this area to settle, they'd thought it was a safe neighborhood.

Their dream come true—a cute little house with a white picket fence.

Now Joe might be dead.

Nothing else mattered except saving her daughter.

CHAPTER 1

Texas Ranger Sergeant Mitchell Manning hammered the *For Sale* sign by the mailbox of his ranch, anxious to get rid of the place.

At one time this ranch had been his life.

His dreams all wrapped up in horses and land and wide-open spaces. A place for his son to run and play, to climb trees and fences, and bond with the Texas land just as he had as a kid.

But now his son and wife were dead, there was nothing left here but memories.

Memories of good times and bad. Memories that haunted him at night and tormented him during the day with the fact that he'd failed them.

They had died because of his damn job.

No more.

He was done with being a Ranger. Done with relationships. Done with wanting anything but the next bottle of whiskey.

Desperate to bury the pain, he forced himself to block out the image of his six-year-old nailing the finishing touches on the tree house they'd built together around the big oak tree.

Instead, he scrutinized the house and his property with a buyer's eye. The rotting boards on the porch needed repairing, the overgrown bushes and weeds tending. As much as he didn't want to be here, he needed to spruce the place up to entice some other sucker to sink their money into it and relieve him of ownership.

But not tonight.

Tonight his best friend Jack Daniels was calling.

Yanking his Stetson down to block the sunlight as it dipped below the horizon, he strode toward his pickup truck. He climbed in, shifted into gear and drove toward the cabin on the creek side.

The rustic log cabin had been built for the foreman of the ranch when his grandparents owned the property, but he'd moved into it now, unable to stand the sounds of the empty farmhouse and Todd's voice echoing through the lonely rooms.

"Daddy, Daddy, Daddy . . ."

Tears burned the backs of his eyelids. He knuckled them away with a curse. Had Todd called out his name when he'd been dying?

Probably. But he'd been unconscious and hadn't heard him. Hadn't saved him.

Christmas music blared from the speakers of the radio,

making him even more surly. Dammit to hell, he didn't want to hear about reindeer and holiday wishes and Santa Claus.

They reminded him too much of his son.

Todd had asked for a new fishing rod and reel this year.

But Todd wouldn't be here to get it, and he would never go fishing again.

Mitch flipped off the radio, but the silence was just as bad, so he focused on the rumbling of his truck as he bounced over the rutted dirt road leading to the cabin. A dark cloud rolled across the sky, adding a gloomy gray to the horizon as he climbed out, grabbed his brown bag and strode to the front porch.

His stomach growled, reminding him he should eat, but he dropped into the chair on the porch, opened the fifth of whiskey, turned it up and downed a hefty swallow.

Maybe his luck would turn around, and he'd end up in the ground beside his son soon.

KAYLIE STARED OUT INTO the night, the Christmas lights glittering along the street bringing a pang to her chest.

It had been almost a year since she'd lost Joe.

Her husband had died trying to protect her and CeCe.

Unable to return to the house after the shooting and during the months afterward, she'd moved to a temporary rental house.

But a few weeks ago, the man who'd killed her husband had escaped prison, and now she and her daughter were in their third safe house in weeks.

With Christmas around the corner, they both wanted to be decorating, shopping and trimming the tree.

But who knew if they would still be here on Christmas?

Besides, they'd been given strict orders to lay low, not to be seen in public or attract attention.

Poor CeCe should be in kindergarten, making friends, finger painting, and singing songs.

Instead, she was immersed in protective custody and struggling with the nightmares of her father's murder.

Damn Larry Buckham for ruining their lives. Kaylie had testified against him, cementing his life sentence in prison.

The district attorney had also made the case that Buckham had terrorized and killed three other families in the same manner. They'd dubbed the serial killer the Family Man. When the jury realized that connection, they hadn't hesitated to convict.

Kaylie and CeCe were the only ones who'd survived his attack.

Unfortunately, Buckham had broken out of prison with two other inmates, and now he was most likely looking to finish her off.

Kaylie glanced at the calendar. One more week until Christmas. Hopefully, Buckham would be back in jail where he belonged by then, and she and CeCe could go home.

Home? Where was that?

Not the little house with the white picket fence where they'd once felt safe. Not with Joe's blood and the stench of his death still permeating the walls and carpet.

The cleaners had assured her they'd gotten out the stains,

but the blood would always be there in Kaylie's mind, tainting the house.

In a few days, Christmas would have come and gone. She would have missed the chance to give CeCe a bright spot in the dismal existence that had become their life.

CeCe looked up from the floor where she lay drawing a picture, her freckles dancing across her pug nose. Kaylie's heart squeezed when she noticed the Christmas tree CeCe had drawn. Only it was bare of decorations and lights, and there were no presents beneath it.

The policeman guarding them, a chuffy guy named Arnold, frowned as his phone buzzed. He snatched it up and paced while he took the call.

As if it wasn't nerve-wracking enough to be locked up for days, he was notorious for pacing, making noises beneath his breath and chewing his nails which only added to her agitation.

Suddenly something blasted through the front window. CeCe jumped up and screamed.

Smoke sizzled from a pipe bomb on the floor.

"Out the back!" the guard yelled.

Kaylie snatched her purse then dragged CeCe through the hall to the kitchen. Smoke began filling the house as they ran for the back door. Behind her, a loud noise sounded, then an explosion shook the walls and floor.

Arnold shouldered his way past her and opened the back door, but a gunshot blasted the air, and he collapsed.

Dear God, it had been a setup.

Terrified, she clutched CeCe behind her. Arnold managed

to lift his hand and fired a round into the man waiting to ambush them. The man cursed and fell backward. Kaylie didn't wait to see if anyone was still moving.

She scooped CeCe into her arms and ran for the car Arnold had stashed out back.

"Mommy!" CeCe cried.

"Shh, baby, it's okay. Just buckle up!" Kaylie's hand trembled as she fumbled for the keys in her purse.

CeCe crawled into the back seat, her cries shattering the night as Kaylie jammed the key into the ignition and roared away.

CeCe was tired of running. And she was scared.

Just like her mommy was, although her mommy pretended everything was going to be okay. But her mommy's voice rattled when she talked sometimes, and at night when CeCe was supposed to be asleep, she heard her mommy crying.

CeCe curled herself into a ball in the back of the car and buried her head into her hands. Tears soaked her fingers and dripped down her cheeks.

How could it be okay when her daddy was dead, and someone wanted to kill her and her mommy?

She squeezed her eyes shut, wishing she could forget the way her daddy looked that night. The way the red blood splattered everywhere, and how his face looked white as milk, and how much her mommy had been shaking when they'd runned away.

Her mommy was shaking now and so was she.

And that man, Mr. Arnold, he was dead, too. He had to be. That was what bullets did to people. Even big men like her daddy and Mr. Arnold.

Tires squealed as her mommy took a turn too fast. CeCe jammed her fist to her mouth to keep from screaming as the car bounced and jolted. If they crashed, she might go to Heaven and see her daddy again.

But she didn't want to go to Heaven, not just yet anyway.

Christmas was almost here.

Not that she was going to get any presents. She and Mommy hadn't even gotten a tree.

Mommy said maybe later. They had to be ready to run in a minute, just like tonight.

A tree would be something else they'd leave behind just like they left all her toys and friends and that nice fat cat Lackey that lived next door. He used to sleep by the fence and crawl up on her windowsill and meow at her through the window.

She rubbed her eyes and looked at the front seat, half thinking she'd see the boogeyman that shot her daddy in the car. But all she saw was the dark and the city lights as they drove out of town.

Where was Mommy going?

Would they get another Mr. Arnold to watch them? Would they change their names again?

She didn't want to change her name. She wanted to be CeCe Whittaker and live in a real house and hang lights on a tree and put stockings on the mantle and make cookies with sprinkles on them.

She wanted to send Santa a letter and tell him what she wanted for Christmas. Not much. Not dozens of toys like she'd asked for last year when she was just a kid. Just four.

All she wanted this year was a real home. Her mommy and daddy together and to get hugs and kisses when she went to bed at night.

Oh, yeah. She wanted a kitty, too. A baby kitten with soft fur and orange hair like fat Lackey.

A kitty to keep her warm and curl up on her pillow and meow, and chase away the boogeyman at night.

But she wouldn't get a kitty this year cause even if Santa got her letter, he wouldn't know where to leave it.

THE DAMN POLICE WERE everywhere looking for him.

Of course, some of them were his friends.

And they had helped him find where little miss Kaylie and her kid were hiding out. But that fat idiot cop had gotten in the way.

So, he'd had to kill him. And now the woman had escaped.

Not for long though.

He steered the car his buddy had left for him through the suburbs, maintaining a low speed to keep from drawing attention to himself as two police cars barreled down the street and whirled into the driveway of the safe house.

Laughter gurgled in his throat.

Safehouse—what a farce.

Kaylie Whittaker and her little girl were anything but safe.

CHAPTER 2

THE CHEAP MOTEL LIGHTS blinked neon green against the dark as Kaylie parked. Her poor little girl had cried for miles and miles until she'd finally fallen asleep from exhaustion.

Kaylie had kept driving until she felt herself starting to nod off, then decided she had to stop for both their sakes. Thankfully, Arnold had stowed some cash in the car along with emergency supplies and insisted she keep an overnight bag for her and CeCe inside, too, in case they had to leave in a hurry.

She'd hoped that wouldn't happen, but here they were on the run again.

She pulled the car around to the back of the motel to prevent it from being seen from the road. Weary from the drive and the night's ordeal, she carried CeCe inside, then eased her down onto the double bed, slipped her shoes off and pulled the covers up over her.

Guilt and anger suffused her as she studied her daughter's tear-swollen face. Guilt for dragging CeCe around the country instead of giving her the safe, loving, stable home she needed. And anger that they were in this situation.

She hurriedly locked the door to the room, shoved a chair against it and collapsed onto the other bed, fatigue clawing at her. But self-preservation kicked in, and she dug the throwaway cell Arnold had given her from her purse.

Who should she call?

No one was supposed to know about the safe house. But somehow Larry Buckham had found them.

How? Had he paid off a cop?

That was the only logical explanation. Arnold had warned her the first time they'd been forced to switch locations that they suspected a leak from the inside.

And now Arnold had been shot . . . Was he dead?

She fiddled with the radio, found a news station, and listened as the reporter detailed a list of crimes across Texas.

"Two of the prisoners who escaped the state pen—Geoffrey Jones and Robert Simpleton—have been apprehended, but forty-year-old Larry Buckham is still at large. Citizens are advised to be on the lookout for the man as he is considered armed and dangerous."

A shiver rippled through Kaylie. She could still see his menacing eyes as he'd glared at her when she took the witness stand. Saw his mouth moving with the promise that he'd kill her if she testified against him.

Because of that threat, she and her daughter had been forced into WITSEC.

The news continued, "A bombing and shooting at a home outside Austin has been reported, one which may be related to Buckham's prison escape. A federal marshal, Arnold Pinter, was shot and killed in the suburban house. Authorities believe that Pinter was protecting a woman named Kaylie Whittaker and her young daughter. Mrs. Whittaker testified at Buckham's trial, stating that he murdered her husband Joe in a home invasion.

"New evidence has just come to light suggesting that Mrs. Whittaker actually murdered her husband and falsely identified Buckham for the crime. Buckham was thought to be the notorious Family Man who murdered three families in their homes, but Buckham's attorney claims she was on the verge of an appeal and had evidence that Buckham did not kill Joe Whittaker or the other families, that he was set up for the crimes.

"Mrs. Whittaker is now wanted for questioning in the case and is considered a person of interest in the death of Marshall Pinter as well."

Kaylie's chest constricted. What? The police thought she killed Joe and now Arnold? That Larry Buckham was innocent?

Hadn't they seen the menacing way he'd looked at her during the trial? Hadn't they heard him threaten to kill her?

For God's sake . . . Larry Buckham was not innocent.

Terrified, she went to the window and pulled the curtain back, just enough to look outside. Two other cars were parked in back. Other than that, the motel was deserted.

Set off the beaten path, the wilderness beckoned. A wilderness that would be a good place to hide.

Anxiety knotted her stomach, and she dug the business card for her WITSEC contact from her purse. The number she was supposed to call if she was in trouble.

Her fingers shook as she punched the number into her cell phone. A machine picked up, and she identified herself according to the code she and Marshal Rafferty had arranged.

Headlights from the highway flickered by as an eighteen-wheeler roared past the motel.

A second later, her call went through.

"I'm sorry, Kaylie," a voice shouted. "Run!"

Rafferty?

Kaylie's heart hammered. "Marshal—"

A gunshot rent the air, then another man's voice. One she'd never forget.

"Hello, Kaylie." A bitter laugh. "Sorry but Marshal Rafferty's done talking."

Kaylie's knees buckled, and she gripped the window ledge and sank into the chair beside it. Dear God, no.

It was Larry Buckham. He'd killed the only person she knew to turn to.

She and Kaylie were on their own now.

MITCH SPENT THE MORNING repairing fencing around the ranch, and the afternoon redoing and painting the front porch of the farmhouse. While he left the porch to dry, he went inside and began cleaning out the closet in the master bedroom.

He was tempted to hire a service to pack up Sally's and Todd's things, but somehow it seemed wrong to allow strangers to touch their belongings. Hell, it seemed wrong for him to touch them, especially to box them up as if he was erasing them from his life.

Not that Sally had really moved in. At least not to stay.

She'd hated the ranch, had wanted to live in the city. She'd been disgusted that the farmhouse needed fixing up and angry that he expected her to settle down in what she called the boring wilderness. She'd begrudgingly moved a few clothes in but had refused to stay in the house until he refurbished it.

Todd had loved the ranch though, had been eager to fish in the creek and learn to ride.

Todd . . . the bright spot in a dull marriage that had disintegrated due to the differences between him and Sally.

Todd . . . the future he'd looked forward to.

Dammit. His son had been taken from him so abruptly he'd never even gotten to say good-bye.

Scrubbing a fist over his bleary eyes, he boxed up Sally's clothes, shoes, and purses and carried them out the back door to his pickup. He cleared out the jewelry box next, grimacing that he'd never been able to afford to buy her diamonds.

But his job as a Ranger hadn't brought the big bucks. At first, she'd said it hadn't mattered, but eventually, she'd longed for expensive, fancy clothes and precious gems, items her rich father had spoiled her with.

And then the trouble had begun. She'd wanted him to quit the Rangers and take a job with her dad. He had refused.

Being a Ranger was who he was. *What* he was.

Or it used to be.

Not anymore.

He stuffed the jewelry box inside a larger box, then tossed in Sally's winter scarves, belts, hats, and shawls. That box went in the truck, too. He tackled the dining room and packed up the fancy doilies, lace tablecloths and ridiculously expensive napkin rings she'd purchased.

None of them fit the ranch house. That should have been a sign that they weren't meant to be together. That she'd wanted another life.

Guilt hammered at him. She'd lost hers because of him.

He should have been the one to die instead of her and Todd.

God, he wished he had.

Last night's binge had dehydrated him, so he went to the kitchen, filled a glass with water and chugged it. Outside, storm clouds threatened, the wind swirling leaves and sticks across the parched grass.

Once he'd wanted to fill that pasture with horses.

Now the pasture was almost as empty as his heart. He'd only kept two ranch horses and the chestnut named Horseshoe that Todd loved so much.

Aching with the memories, he forced himself to go to Todd's room. Pain knifed through him at the sight of the toys his son had played with. Sally had decorated the room in a baseball theme, and her father had started a baseball card collection with Todd.

Even though the old man hated Mitch now, he had loved his

grandson. Mitch packed the baseball cards and other baseball paraphernalia into a box and labeled it to mail to Sally's father.

He boxed Todd's clothes next, his heartbreaking at the reality that his son would never wear his favorite rawhide jacket or cowboy boots again. Mitch didn't realize he was crying until he felt the tears drip down his cheek.

He swiped at them, then carried the boxes to the truck, determined to take care of them that day. But when he returned to Todd's room and saw the stuffed toys, farm animals, horses and stable that his son had collected, anguish threatened to break him.

On the shelf beside the bed sat Todd's rock collection. One of Todd's favorite things to do was skip stones across the pond. He'd collected the smooth, odd shaped rocks as if they were treasures.

Unable to part with them, he boxed the stones to take to his cabin, then packed the toys in another box and slipped them under the bed out of sight. One day he'd donate them to a children's shelter or hospital, but for now, they were all he had left of his son.

That and the picture he kept in his wallet. He pulled it out, traced a finger over his little boy's innocent face, and headed out the back to meet his best friend Jack.

***

KAYLIE WAITED UNTIL DARK, then ushered CeCe back into the car again. Knowing the police were looking for her made traveling during daylight more dangerous.

It also meant that she had to ditch the car Arnold had commandeered for them.

She found a used car lot on the outskirts of a little town called Twin Branches and talked the owner into trading it for a Pathfinder. Using the fake ID Arnold had given her helped, but she needed to ditch that as well.

If someone on the inside killed Arnold and Rafferty, they might know her new name.

"Mommy, where are we going?" CeCe asked.

Kaylie sighed, weary of running. She wanted to sugarcoat the situation for her daughter, but CeCe would see through a lie.

"I don't know, honey. Mommy's trying to make a plan."

CeCe sniffled. "I wanna go home."

There was that word again. *Home*?

But they didn't have a home now, and no telling when they would. Not until Buckham was caught.

And until she cleared her name.

Another problem added to the mounting pile.

Being a real estate agent had not prepared her for a life on the run.

Christmas lights twinkled along the street signs in Twin Branches, the storefronts decorated with Santas and snowmen, even though it rarely snowed in this part of Texas.

Holiday music wafted from speakers in town and stores, and the toy store and pet shop advertised specials featuring the latest gift ideas. Puppies and kittens were also half priced.

"Mommy, look," CeCe said. "They have kitties in the store."

"I see, honey," Kaylie said.

"Can we stop and get one?"

A pang tugged at Kaylie's chest. "Not today, CeCe. But maybe soon, once we're settled back down."

"But I want one now," CeCe said, a pout forming on her mouth.

"I understand you do," Kaylie said. "But, sweetie, kitties don't travel well."

CeCe folded her arms. "I'm never gonna get one cause all we do is drive and drive and go and go and go."

Kaylie gripped the steering wheel. "I'm sorry, honey. I'm doing the best I can."

CeCe pulled her legs up and propped her folded arms on top of them. "Santa won't ever find me if we don't gots a house."

Kaylie battled tears. "Santa will find you. I promise."

But CeCe settled into a pout that wouldn't lift. Kaylie could hardly blame her. She hated running herself and was terrified for their lives.

Poor CeCe's world had completely crumbled in a matter of minutes.

A *For Rent* sign on one of the buildings caught her eye, and she had an idea. Properties rarely sold or were bought during the holidays.

Which meant that properties weren't being shown, owners were too busy with families to check on business, and houses were sitting empty.

She checked the storefronts and discovered a real estate office on the corner. Anxious to see what she could find, she parked in front of the office.

"Stay here," she told CeCe.

CeCe forgot her pout and sat up, straining to see what her mother was doing as Kaylie slid from the car, snatched one of the free real estate magazines from the display in front of the office, then jumped back in the car.

She shifted, backed out and drove out of town, then stopped at a hamburger joint. She drove through the drive-in and ordered food, then pulled to the back of the dimly lit parking lot and parked.

Happy again, CeCe devoured her burger and fries, then entertained herself, temporarily satisfied with the toy she'd received with her meal, while Kaylie scoured the pages of the real estate magazine.

There were two apartments and three houses listed in town. It would be chancy to squat in a place close to residents and businesses where people might see her coming and going and get suspicious. She needed a place out of town, maybe on a deserted road, someplace no one would look or visit, at least until after the holidays ended.

Two different ads caught her eye, one for a Victorian house that actually boasted that it was haunted.

A shiver went up her spine. She and her daughter had enough ghosts haunting them to last a lifetime.

The next—a ranch for sale about ten miles out of town. It was called the Double M, the ad sporting two M's intertwined.

It had just gone on the market.

That was the kind of place she needed, a house off the grid. But what if someone was still living there?

There was only one way to find out.

She turned onto the road and headed toward the ranch.

THE GUNSHOT PIERCED MITCH'S chest, knocking the breath out of him.

Sally screamed. "Mitch!"

"Daddy!" Todd cried from the backseat.

"I'm okay," he muttered, although he wasn't okay. He'd been hit and was bleeding out fast. And the goon that had shot him raced up and slammed the side of his vehicle with his truck.

Tires screeched as Mitch swerved. Sally tried to grab the steering wheel, but the Jeep skimmed the guardrail and spun out of control. Mitch pumped the brakes, but they were going too fast, and the SUV crashed through the rail and careened toward the river.

Sally screamed again.

Mitch clenched the steering wheel as the Jeep nosedived into the water. Then everything went black.

CHAPTER 3

M ITCH JERKED AWAKE, PANTING and sweating, the nightmare so vivid that he heard his wife and son's screams as if they were in the car that second.

But they were gone.

Grief and sorrow clenched his chest.

He rubbed his hand over his eyes, then absentmindedly over the scar on his chest. The doctors assured him he wasn't to blame, that he'd tried to get his little boy and wife out, but they'd been trapped, and he'd been so weak that he'd lost consciousness from blood loss at the edge of the river.

How could he not blame himself? It was his fault they'd died.

If he could have traded his life for theirs, he would have in a second.

Emotions pummeled him, making bile rise to his throat. God . . . *why* had he lived?

Was this God's way of punishing him for not being a better man? Not being a better husband? Not spending enough time with his son?

The week before the shooting, Todd had begged Mitch to take him fishing, but Mitch had been adamant about finishing his latest case. A sadistic man named Maurice Willingham had shot and killed two men, but escaped detection.

Until Mitch had convinced Willingham's wife to turn on him.

He'd made the arrest, proud that he'd finally locked the man up.

Willingham had hated Mitch for that and vowed retribution.

Shockingly, the bastard had made bail. As he walked out of jail, he'd promised to make Mitch suffer.

Mitch had understood the warning. Fearing Sally and Todd were in danger, he'd raced home, ushered them in the car so he could protect them.

But Willingham had help, an accomplice who'd followed Mitch and fired that bullet into Mitch's chest.

Thunder rumbled outside, accompanied by the sound of horses whinnying. He should have put them in the barn earlier.

His mouth tasted gritty and dry from the Jack Daniels, and his head was pounding like a jackhammer was beating behind his eyes. He reached for some aspirin and water but thought he heard an engine rumble in the distance.

Who the hell would be coming out to the Double M this

time of night?

Curious, he rolled off the bed, staggering as he shuffled across the room, grabbed his rifle and walked outside.

From the front porch of the cabin which sat on a hill over-looking the ranch, he could make out the farmhouse in the distance. A few stars fought through the storm clouds, glittering against the inky darkness, the moon a sliver of pale gold light.

But twin beams from an SUV flashed across the land, then died as the car rolled to a stop. Mitch's detective instincts surged to life.

He'd just put the ranch on the market. Had some teens seen the ad and decided to use the place as a party house?

Then again, one of the prison escapees was still on the loose.

He propped his rifle by the side of the door, stepped inside, grabbed his night binoculars, walked back onto the porch, and peered through the lenses to see what was going on.

The driver's door opened, a pair of jean-clad legs emerging.

A woman's legs, he realized, as that sliver of moonlight streaked her golden hair.

Mitch's gut tightened. She was a tiny little thing. Was she lost?

She stood by the car and glanced in all directions, craning to see up the dirt drive as if she was looking for someone. Then she leaned inside the car and removed a pistol.

Clutching it to her, she eased her way around to the side of the farmhouse near the carport, again searching the area.

If she'd seen the ad regarding the sale, why would she come out here in the middle of the night to look at the house?

And why was she carrying a gun?

Returning to the front of the house, she climbed the porch steps, once again glancing around, except this time he saw the expression in her eyes and realized she was nervous.

She peered through the windows, then tiptoed toward the front door and tried it. She looked frustrated that it wouldn't open.

Rubbing at her shoulders as if she was tired, she walked around to the side of the house, jiggled a window, then another. The lock on the laundry room window was broken, and she pushed it open.

Carefully she tucked the gun into the waist of her jeans, hoisted herself up and crawled through the window to the inside.

Mitch scowled as suspicions kicked in. She was breaking into his house? Why? There was nothing to steal.

A second later, a light flipped on in the hallway, then she exited through the front door. Anger rose inside him, and he reached for his rifle.

He didn't care who the hell she was. He was going to tell her to get the hell out of his house.

He headed down the steps, keeping the binoculars trained on her. Dust blew in the air as the storm clouds kicked in.

The woman ran to the back door of the Pathfinder, opened it, and scooped up a little girl in her arms

Mitch's heart stuttered at the sight of the sleeping child, stopping him in his tracks. The towheaded nymph curled against the woman, one hand clutching a rag doll, the other a little plastic train.

The woman hurried inside with the child, flicking another light on in the foyer as she found her way up the stairs. When Todd's light flickered on, Mitch's chest squeezed with a sharp pang.

She was putting the little girl to bed in his son's room.

Seconds later, she ran outside, got in the car, started it and drove it around to the back of the farmhouse where it was hidden from the road.

Whatever the woman had done, or whatever she was running from—and it was obvious that she was running and scared—he couldn't confront her tonight. Not when that little girl looked so innocent.

He'd find out what was going on first, then he'd decide what to do about his unwanted guests.

KAYLIE DRAGGED HER SUITCASE and CeCe's pink Cinderella bag up the stairs to the bedrooms. Guilt niggled at her for invading another person's home, but as far as she could tell from her brief run through the house, no one was living here.

There were no clothes or personal items anywhere, not in the closets or bedrooms. No groceries in the kitchen or refrigerator either, indicating no one had been here in a while.

She wondered who owned the ranch. A number was listed in the paper but no real estate agency, so it must be for sale by owner.

Her shoulders ached as she dropped CeCe's bag in the

smaller bedroom. The room was painted a deep blue suggesting it had been a boy's room at one time. CeCe wouldn't care.

Her daughter just needed a warm bed and safe place to sleep.

And they both needed a break from running.

Hope budded as she rolled her suitcase into the other bedroom. Maybe they could lay low here until after the holidays, and she could give CeCe a real Christmas.

Surely by then, the police would have Buckham back in custody. Although the news reporter said his attorney had evidence he was innocent...And why did they suspect that she'd hurt Joe?

Her head swirled with ugly possibilities. What was she going to do? Arnold was dead and Rafferty might be, too. Who could she turn to for help?

Sick with worry, she hurried down the stairs and locked the house, then tiptoed back to the second floor, carrying her gun to the bedside table. The antique four-poster bed and dresser reminded her of her grandmother's house, stirring a sense of nostalgia for lost family and the future she'd thought she and Joe had built together.

That life was gone.

Wiping at tears, she fought the memory of Joe's funeral. It seemed like she was destined to bury everyone she loved. She'd lost her parents at seventeen, her grandmother at twenty and now her husband.

She could not lose her little girl.

Determination made her grind her teeth. CeCe didn't

deserve any of this, not watching her father die or living on the run or being scared all the time.

Somehow she had to make it up to her.

The bed had been stripped of sheets, but she dug into a closet in the master bathroom, found a set of plain white ones and made the bed.

Exhausted, she tucked the pistol under her pillow, stripped her clothes, tugged on pajamas and crawled into bed. Thunder rumbled outside, the sound of a light rain splattering against the roof of the house.

Tomorrow she'd figure out a way to clear her name.

Tonight she had to get some sleep.

She closed her eyes, grateful for a reprieve from the road. But instead of sugar plum fairies, reindeer and tree trimming, images of dead bodies—Joe's, then Arnold's—danced through her head.

Then her own . . .

She shut out the image. She couldn't die or go to jail for a crime she hadn't committed.

She had to survive to take care of CeCe.

MITCH TRIED TO SLEEP, but questions about the woman who'd invaded his house needled him, and he walked outside for air.

He didn't like them there, not in the home he'd made for his own family.

Yet the woman looked scared. For God's sake, she'd snuck

inside in the middle of the damn night with a gun as if she was running for her life.

Or from the law.

Still, how could he force them to leave when he didn't know if she was a criminal—or if she and the little girl were in danger.

He'd failed his own wife and son.

The reminder nearly sent him to his knees. He clutched the porch rail, fighting the grief eating him inside out. How could he keep breathing when every fiber of his being was on fire with pain?

He glanced back at the farmhouse, the horses finally settling down and quieting as they hovered near the barn.

Dammit to hell. He didn't need to take on someone else's troubles. This woman and her kid were not his problem.

Yes, they are. They're in your house.

The question was why?

A dozen different scenarios rolled through his head. Maybe they were just traveling and ran out of money and needed a place to sleep for one night. The lady could be in financial trouble. Or hell, someone could have stolen her credit cards and wallet and she couldn't very well drive all night, and she was just trying to get back to family.

She might have a husband or boyfriend somewhere waiting on them.

Hopefully, she'd hightail it out come dawn, and he could forget about her and that little girl with the rag doll and that little plastic train toy.

The child had freckles on her nose. He'd seen them through

the binoculars as she'd hugged up to her mother.

Hugged up to her the way Todd used to hug him when he had a bad dream during the night.

Todd had loved trains and toy animals and his cowboy boots. Sometimes at night, he slid in bed beside Mitch, and Mitch told him stories about camping out, roasting marshmallows and hunting arrowheads on the ranch.

He'd promised to take Todd camping, but they'd never gotten the chance. Todd had died two days before they'd planned to leave. Their bedrolls had been packed, camping gear stashed in the back of the Jeep when they'd crashed.

The crime scene photos had shown marshmallows floating in the river beside Todd's body.

Mitch would never be able to erase that image from his head.

A streak of lightning zigzagged across the top of the trees surrounding the house, illuminating the window of the master bedroom.

Sorrow and regret mingled with anger at the damn woman for making him feel again. For making him worry about someone when all he wanted was to drown his grief in a bottle until he was so numb he'd never feel anything again.

He strode inside and reached for the bottle of whiskey, but when he glanced up at the ranch house and saw a light flicker on in the master bedroom—in *his* bedroom—and watched the silhouette of the woman pacing the room, rubbing her arms and wringing her hands together, he set the bottle back down.

He didn't know what her story was, but he'd damn well find

out. And he needed a clear head to deal with her when he ran her off in the morning because he had a weakness for a woman and kid in trouble.

And he was *not* falling into that trap again.

———•———

CeCe stirred from sleep and opened her eyes, squinting to see where she was.

In a bedroom somewhere. The last thing she remembered was her mommy driving to a ranch with horse stables and saying they'd spend the night in the house.

A whisper made her roll sideways, and she clenched the sheet. A boy with dark hair was standing by the window in jeans, a T-shirt and cowboy hat.

She bit her lip to keep from screaming. "Who are you?" she managed to whisper.

"Todd," the boy said. "You're sleeping in my bed."

CeCe's stomach started to hurt. "My mommy said no one lives here."

"I do," Todd said.

But he was floating away like he was on a cloud, and CeCe couldn't see him anymore.

"Take care of my horse," the boy said as he slipped away.

CeCe hugged the pillow to her. She had to be dreaming. But just in case she wasn't, and the boy really did have a horse here, she promised him she would.

———·———

"DID YOU FIND THE Whittaker woman?"

"I'm on her trail. She ditched the car Pinter was using and traded it for a Pathfinder. I'm looking for it now."

"Find her. I am not going to prison."

Hell. He didn't intend to go back either. "Don't worry. I'll take care of the broad."

"Good. This past year has been a fucking nightmare."

He punched disconnect then turned to his attorney Willa Barnaby and stripped his clothes, eager to plant himself inside her.

She dropped her silk blouse to the floor, licking her lips in invitation.

He ripped off her bra and cradled her big breasts in his hands. "I've missed you, sweetheart."

She rubbed a hand over his cock, making it harden even more. "I missed you, too."

He flicked his tongue over one ripe nipple, furious at Kaylie Whittaker for depriving him of his freedom and the pleasures that went with it the past few months.

Her husband had gotten exactly what he'd deserved.

And soon she would, too.

Then his problems would be over.

And he could screw Willa any time he damn well wanted.

CHAPTER 4

Mitch felt like a voyeur the next morning as he peered through his binoculars to study the house, but he had to find out what the woman was up to. By dawn, he'd begun to wonder if she was holed up meeting someone or if perhaps she was running from an abusive spouse.

That was the logical explanation. He'd seen the same sad story too many times to count. Women dependent on some jackass who used and abused them, then made them think they were to blame. Men who should have their own butts kicked and their faces smashed in for venting his anger and small-mindedness on women and children too small to defend themselves.

Of course, she could be a money-hungry princess who'd stolen the man's child just to exhort cash from her husband. Hell, he'd seen that scenario, too.

In both situations, the kid suffered the most.

That little strawberry blonde girl with the freckles tugged at his damn heart. A heart he'd thought had broken beyond feeling anything but pain.

He slipped into the barn, saddled up Horseshoe, the chestnut Todd had loved, and rode across the ranch, searching for anything suspicious.

Or someone who might be meeting with the blonde at the house.

But his search turned up empty. Although in the north pasture, he spotted a truck sitting high on the hill. But when he nudged Horseshoe in that direction, the truck barreled off.

That raised his suspicions, so he rode the property again, then circled back and steered the horse to drink from the creek while he dismounted and watched the farmhouse from the hill.

Hoping the woman and kid would leave first thing, he forced himself to wait instead of confronting her. He'd give her time to get off his land on her own.

He just hoped to hell she did. Then he could avoid asking questions and entrenching himself deeper into her life.

Finally, as daylight fought through the winter clouds, she emerged from the house. She wore a long-sleeved pink T-shirt and jeans that hugged curves, curves he hadn't noticed last night in the dark. She'd pulled her long blonde hair into a ponytail, drawing it back from her face, which accentuated high cheekbones and a pouty little sweet mouth.

Sweet as in her lips were plump like raspberries and stirred a man's blood with the desire to kiss her.

Dammit.

Out pranced little Miss Sunshine with the freckles, her own strawberry blonde ponytail swinging as she clutched that scraggly doll to her. Her eyes lit up when she spotted the horses trotting across the pasture.

For the love of Christ.

The mother and daughter could have passed for angels had he not seen the pistol in the woman's hands and the fear in her eyes the night before.

The woman stooped down and cradled her daughter's face between her hands then said something to her that made the little girl burst into a big smile.

Mitch cursed and prayed they were leaving for good as they hurried around back to their SUV.

***

KAYLIE SCANNED THE DIRT road as she drove toward the small town she'd passed through the night before. She needed coffee, food, and a plan.

She could find the first two in Twin Branches, but the third one stumped her.

"I'm hungry," CeCe said from the back seat.

"Me, too, baby," Kaylie said. "We're going to get something to eat in town."

"I wanna go back to the ranch," CeCe said. "Did you see the horses?"

"Yes, I did." Nerves twisted Kaylie's stomach. The horses

were beautiful. But keeping livestock on the land meant that someone would most likely come out to take care of them.

"Can I ride one of the horsies?"

She doubted that would happen. "I don't know. We'll see."

"That means no," CeCe said with her infamous stubborn pout.

Kaylie tossed a smile over her shoulder. "That means we'll see. First, we're going to get a big breakfast, then pick up some groceries."

"You mean we really are gonna stay at the ranch?"

Kaylie swallowed hard at the unbridled hope in her daughter's voice. "For a little while maybe." Unless the owner comes by and catches us squatting.

"Can I get a kitty, too?"

Kaylie laughed. "Breakfast and groceries first. We'll have to talk to Santa about the kitty." And wait until we're not running for our lives.

"Okay, but I wants pancakes with chocolate chip eyes."

"Sounds good," Kaylie said as she entered the town square. With its old-fashioned storefronts, small grocery store, boot store and diner boasting homemade barbeque, Twin Branches could have been any other little hole-in-the-wall town in Texas. Still, there was something charming and quaint about it that made Kaylie relax.

Two women strolling their babies crossed the street to a park in the center of town, an elderly man and woman held hands as they entered the diner, and two men in overalls sat on the front porch of the general store playing checkers over a whiskey barrel.

A discount store was beside the diner, and she made a note to check it out for disguises for her and CeCe in case they needed to change their appearance.

She parked in front of the diner, tugged a baseball cap over her head, then tossed CeCe a cap. The two of them joined hands and hurried to the door.

Still, she kept glancing over her shoulder, scanning the street and diner as they entered, praying no one was following them.

MITCH SNUCK INTO THE farmhouse, irritated that he felt as if he was a thief in the night and that he was violating the woman's privacy when *she* was the one who'd broken into *his* house.

He glanced around the kitchen and living room, noting everything looked as he'd left it. Sheets draped over furniture, bare kitchen counter, curtains drawn. For the first time, he saw the place as his wife had.

Dusty, rundown, in need of a good cleaning and decent furniture.

Although Sally had wanted to gut the place, he'd insisted the wood floors and crown moldings were timeless.

He wondered what the stranger in his house thought. And if she was coming back.

He hadn't seen her lugging her suitcase to the car when she'd left.

Which meant she'd return for them any minute.

He had to hurry.

Grumbling beneath his breath, he climbed the steps to the second floor, his boots pounding. He paused at the top of the stairwell to look in his son's room and saw the bed was made, although that damn doll with the ratty dress and scraggly orange hair lay on the pillow as if it had found a home.

Hell, yeah. They'd be back. The kid would have taken the doll with her if they were leaving for good. Just what were the woman's plans?

Something tugged at his heart, emotions he didn't want to feel, and he cursed and strode to the master bedroom—*his* room. Sally had hated the outdated curtains and antiques, but he'd admired the craftsmanship of the four-poster shaker-style bed. Besides, a painting of mustangs hung above the bed, a reminder of his passion for ranch life, open spaces and taming wild horses.

He'd expected to find peace and tranquility here but instead had lost everything. Now the ranch just felt plain lonely.

The woman had made the bed up and put her suitcase on top of the chaise in the corner. He bypassed it and checked the bathroom, the faint scent of lavender swirling in the air, a feminine smell that sent a jolt of awareness through him.

A travel-size shampoo and conditioner sat in the shower caddy, a small make-up bag on the bathroom vanity.

An image of the blonde naked in his shower taunted him.

Banishing the image, he returned to the bedroom and rummaged through her suitcase, looking for information about his guest. The suitcase held another pair of jeans, two T-shirts, and three long sleeved shirts, all in various pastel shades.

Beneath the pile of clothes, he found lingerie—satin and lace panties and bras that were so sexy they made his cock harden.

Damn, he was pathetic if underwear was turning him on. The last thing he needed was to lust after any woman, much less one in trouble.

Especially one with a kid.

That path was too dangerous.

He carefully tried to place the garments back as she'd left them, then unzipped the zipper pouch on the outside of the bag.

His pulse hammered. This was what he was looking for—some kind of ID.

Only when he opened the manila envelope, out slid a wad of cash and three different pieces of identification.

All with pictures of the stranger in his house. All three boasting different names.

Tammy Langley. Collette Watts. Loretta Cagle.

The gut instincts that came with his job surged to life. What the hell was going on?

Could she possibly be in WITSEC? Or was she an identity thief, or a criminal using different IDs to escape being apprehended?

———

"CeCe, honey, I hate to do this, but if anyone asks here in town, my name is Kat."

CeCe scrunched her nose into a frown. "Who am I going to be, Mommy?"

Kaylie sipped her coffee. When they'd first gone into hiding, she'd presented the fake names as a game. At first, CeCe had thought it was fun.

But it was wearing on both of them.

"Who do you want to be?"

CeCe chewed a forkful of pancakes. "I wants to be CeCe and go back to the ranch with the horsies and make sprinkle cookies for Santa Claus."

Kaylie ached that she couldn't give that to her. "I know. Just a little longer, baby, and I'll figure out how to make that happen." The door opened to the diner, and a man in a sheriff's uniform strode in, his gaze sweeping the place.

God, she hoped the police hadn't figured out what kind of car she was driving now. That sheriff might recognize the Pathfinder and detain her.

If he took her in for questioning, she might lose CeCe.

And if Arnold and Rafferty had been killed by someone in law enforcement, turning to him for help could be dangerous.

Kaylie pulled the brim of her hat lower and dipped her head to speak to CeCe. "Finish your breakfast, sweetie. We need to go in a minute."

CeCe swallowed a swig of orange juice then set the glass down with a thunk. "I'll be Dora. Like Dora the Explorer."

Kaylie smiled. "Good thinking. Dora, you can help me explore the town."

CeCe brightened at the idea and gobbled down the rest of her pancakes while Kaylie finished her eggs and coffee. The sheriff bypassed them with only a minor nod of his head.

A second later, he slid in the booth across from them with a tall man with a goatee who raked his gaze over Kaylie with interest. He had long sideburns, a cleft in his chin and a scar below his left eye.

Kaylie tugged her daughter's hand in hers, and they walked to the register to pay. But as she closed her wallet, she sensed someone watching her.

Her skin prickling, she peered sideways through the window as they left, and realized the man with the sheriff was still watching her. Operating on autopilot, she memorized his features. A long face, hazel eyes, black Stetson, western clothing.

Did he work with the sheriff? Did he know who she was? Had Buckham hired him to kill her?

MITCH STEWED OVER HOW to handle the situation as the Pathfinder barreled down the drive toward the farmhouse. From his vantage point on horseback, he watched the SUV come to a stop.

The woman slid out, her long legs unfolding gracefully, then hurried around to help the little girl with her seatbelt. The nymph jumped down from the seat and proceeded to spin in circles as she ran through the grass while her mother unloaded four bags of groceries and carried them inside.

Four bags of groceries meant she was planning to stay longer than one night.

Were they all for her and the child, or was she expecting company?

The little girl started doing cartwheels, her body bouncing and falling as she struggled with them. But she didn't seem to mind that she messed up. Instead, she turned her face up to the sun and danced around again, then belted into an off key chorus of *Rudolph the Red-nosed Reindeer.*

Todd had loved that song, too.

Grief clogged his throat for a moment as he pictured his little boy running through the fields with this freckled-face child.

The woman stepped onto the porch. "Come on inside, honey."

The little girl bent to pick up a rock. "But I wanna stay out here and play."

Her mother shaded her eyes with her hand and stretched, looking down the drive toward the road. "All right, for a few minutes. But if you see a car, run inside."

"'kay!" Another failed cartwheel, and the girl landed on her head. She laughed though as she got up and tried again.

A second later she twirled around and noticed Todd's tree house. She squealed, raced over and climbed the ladder. Mitch's heart skipped a beat. He could still hear Todd laughing as they nailed the wood boards together, craning his neck, shouting that he could see for miles from the top of the oak.

Mitch kicked Horseshoe's sides, sending her into a trot, mentally debating how to approach the intruder.

He couldn't let her know who he was or that he was a Texas Ranger.

Former Texas Ranger.

The chestnut bounded down the hill across the pasture, slowing as they approached the front yard.

The little girl suddenly spotted him, scrambled down and ran for the porch. Her scream sent a shudder through Mitch and made him feel like a heel.

Dammit, he hadn't meant to scare her.

But he wasn't the one trespassing.

Seconds later, the screened door opened, and the woman stepped outside, the little girl clutching the woman's leg as she hid behind her.

He froze, bringing Horseshoe to a halt as she raised a gun and aimed it at his chest.

CHAPTER 5

Kaylie clutched the gun with a white-knuckled grip.

Beside her, she felt CeCe's anxiety. God help her, she hated that her daughter had to be scared. Especially when five minutes ago, she was laughing and turning cartwheels in the grass and singing about Rudolph like a normal five-year-old.

The stranger on the horse slowly raised his hands as if in surrender. "Don't shoot, ma'am. I don't want to hurt you."

Kaylie's hand trembled. "Who are you?"

The tall, rugged cowboy tilted the corner of his black Stetson, his eyes narrowing. Those eyes were coal black. His jaw chiseled and angular. His lips thick and pressed into an angry slash of a line.

Not the man from town.

If she wasn't scared to death, he was there to kill her and CeCe, she'd think he was handsome.

"Name's Mitch, ma'am. What's yours?"

Kaylie tensed, struggling to remember the cover name she'd chosen. "Kat."

"And yours, pumpkin?" Mitch asked with a smile toward CeCe.

CeCe wiggled behind Kaylie. "CeCe."

So much for Dora. CeCe inched one toe up beside Kaylie but still clung to her side.

Mitch's gaze cut toward her daughter, and something akin to pain flashed in his eyes. "I didn't mean to scare you, CeCe."

The breath Kaylie had been holding eased from her chest. If this man was a hired killer, he wouldn't apologize for frightening CeCe. He'd just pull a gun and shoot them.

"That's a pretty name."

CeCe grinned. "My daddy picked it."

"Is your daddy here?" Mitch asked.

CeCe pointed toward the sky and shook her head. "He wents to heaven. Mommy says I can talk to him anytime I want, but I tried and he don't talk back."

Kaylie winced, hoping Mitch would drop the subject.

"I'm sure you miss him," Mitch said. "But I bet he hears everything you say to him."

"What do you want, Mitch?" Kaylie said, unnerved by the big man. She didn't want to have to leave here tonight, but she would if necessary.

"You bought the place?"

Kaylie chewed the inside of her cheek. She couldn't go so far with her fabricated story to declare that she'd bought the ranch.

What if he wanted proof?

"No, we're just staying here for a little while, maybe till the house sells," Kaylie hedged. Unless Buckham found them first.

"Then you're renting?" Mitch asked.

Kaylie shook her head, searching for a plausible explanation. "I'm a real estate agent. Properties show much better if someone's living in them and if they're cleaned up. I thought I'd stay here and spiff up the inside so it would sell after the holidays." She had done that before. Not stayed in the house before, but dressed it up.

"I see." The saddle squeaked in the tension that ensued as Mitch shifted on the horse. "Do you mind putting the gun down, ma'am? You're making me and Horseshoe nervous." He patted the horse's long neck for emphasis.

Horseshoe? Surely a killer wouldn't name his horse Horseshoe.

Still, she couldn't trust anyone.

But she did lower the gun slightly, mostly for CeCe's sake.

Kaylie guarded her words. "Do you know the owner of the ranch?"

The man gave her a long assessing look which made Kaylie want to squirm. But she resisted, determined not to draw attention to herself.

"We never met. But he called me and said he put his place on the market and asked me to come by and do some painting for him, inside and out. Said he planned to be out of touch for a while, but he'd leave me a check at the bank." He hooked his thumb toward the hill on the left. "Said I could stay out in the cabin on the creek."

Kaylie turned in the direction Mitch pointed and spotted a small rustic cabin in the distance. She hadn't realized it was there, but if he was staying in the cabin, he'd probably seen her arrive.

CeCe's nails dug into her jean-clad leg. "Mommy? Can I pet the horsie?"

Kaylie heaved a weary breath, survival instincts urging her to run. But she'd promised CeCe they'd stay another night, and she couldn't bear to break her heart.

But what if this man wasn't who he said he was? What if he was working for Larry Buckham?

Or what if the owner called Mitch, and he found out she'd just told him a pack of lies?

MITCH LIFTED A HAND slowly to make sure he didn't startle the woman. Kat, that's the name she gave, but he'd bet his badge that she was lying.

"I think Horseshoe would like to be petted," he said gently.

The little nymph's eyes lit up, blue eyes like her mother's, he noted, her freckles dancing across the bridge of her nose. But instead of running over, she hesitated and turned her face up to Kat. "Okay, Mommy?"

The tension lining his intruder's face softened, making her look young and vulnerable, and so gorgeous that his chest clanged.

Then she ran a hand over her daughter's hair with such love

that he nearly choked. How many times had he scrubbed his hand over Todd's unruly hair with affection?

Jesus Christ. If every movement the woman and kid made brought a lump to his throat, he had to get them off his property fast.

"Sure, sweetie, just be gentle." Kat tucked the gun into the waistband of her jeans, then took her daughter's hand, and together they walked down the porch steps.

Mitch dismounted and patted Horseshoe's flanks. "Hey buddy, there's someone here that wants to meet you."

CeCe fluttered her hand in a wave to the animal, a simple childlike gesture that touched Mitch again. He held the reigns, keeping the chestnut steady as the little girl stroked his side.

"You want me to lift you up so you can pet his neck?" Mitch asked.

She nodded enthusiastically, dimples flashing. His gaze met Kat's, the wariness in her mother's expression tearing at Mitch.

She was afraid for her daughter?

Why? Had someone hurt CeCe?

Kat's husband? CeCe's father? A boyfriend?

Anger surged through him, but he tamped it down as he lifted the child so she could reach Horseshoe's mane.

She was nothing but a baby in his arms. The idea that someone had hurt her triggered his protective instincts.

"You know animals sense when people are nice and when they love them," he said in a gruff voice. "They sense who they can trust."

His gaze met Kat's again, and a flicker of understanding

appeared in the depths of her bottomless eyes. Eyes that had known fear.

The eyes of a mother who would do anything for her child.

Whatever she might have done at that moment, illegal or not, he didn't care.

He would make sure they were safe from whatever they were running from.

KAYLIE WATCHED HER LITTLE girl pet the horse under the supervision of the cowboy, her heart in her throat.

She'd always believed you could tell a lot about a person by the way they treated animals and children.

He was both commanding with the horse and gentle at the same time, using a low voice to introduce Horseshoe to CeCe. Where his sharp gaze had scrutinized her moments before, those same troubled, dark eyes softened when he looked at her daughter.

"I think he likes you," Mitch said as the horse nuzzled CeCe's palm with his nose.

CeCe giggled. "I like him, too."

The sound of CeCe's laugh made Kaylie ache all over. "He's gentle," she said as she glanced up at the cowboy. "Has he been around kids before?"

The softness in Mitch's eyes vanished, a wall of steel sliding down over his chiseled jaw. He gave a brief nod, then lowered CeCe to the ground. "I guess I should get to work."

CeCe shifted back and forth between her left and right foot. "Can I ride Horseshoe?"

Kaylie could have sworn anguish flashed across Mitch's face. "Not right now, sweet pea."

"Please, please, pretty please with sugar on it," CeCe pleaded.

Kaylie squeezed her daughter's shoulder. "Come on, honey. Mitch said he has work to do, and we're keeping him."

CeCe dug her sneaker into the dirt. "But I wants to ride like a real cowboy."

Kaylie wanted to snap at CeCe for being petulant, but CeCe had been through so much the last few months that she bit back a chiding comment.

Mitch saved her by squatting down to CeCe's eye level. "You be good and help your mommy, then we'll see. Okay?"

CeCe's face brightened. "'kay."

Mitch looked up at Kaylie. "What do you plan to do inside the house?"

Kaylie shrugged. "First I'll give it a thorough cleaning."

"And we're gonna get a Christmas tree and put up decorations," CeCe chimed in.

"Did you plan to paint the inside?" Kaylie asked him.

Mitch swung his big body back up in the saddle. "Do you think it will help sell the place?"

Kaylie nodded. "Yes. I'd use a neutral shade through the house. It'll make it look fresher and make the rooms feel larger."

Mitch tipped his hat. "Then pick out a paint color, and I'll get started after I repair the fencing around the property."

Kaylie pulled CeCe back against her and stroked her arms.

She should have told him no about the painting, but her professional experience wouldn't allow her to lie. Of course, giving the rooms a facelift would make the farmhouse show better.

But could she handle this sexy man inside the house with her and her daughter?

And what if he wasn't who he said he was? Would she and CeCe be safe with him?

***

"Do you know where they are?"

Buckham gripped the phone with a clammy hand. It wasn't supposed to go down like this. He should never have gotten caught. The woman never should have identified him.

And the jury shouldn't have believed her since she'd never seen his face. She'd only heard his voice.

But the bitch had been so convincing with her tears and drama and her story about saving her little girl that those damn twelve strangers had sunk his ass with a guilty verdict. Worse, they thought he was that fucking, sick jerk who was going around killing families.

He almost laughed at the irony. Him a serial killer?

Hardly.

"I asked you if you know where they are."

"I'm close." He could smell it. After all, the woman was an amateur.

And his lawyer had friends in high places.

Soon he would get his revenge.

CHAPTER 6

THE NEXT FEW DAYS Kaylie spent the mornings cleaning the house. CeCe followed her from room to room, chatting about the horses outside and singing Christmas carols while Kaylie dusted, scrubbed, pulled down curtains and washed them. She stripped the throws off the furniture, polished the antiques and mopped the floors, shining them with wood floor cleaner.

CeCe played in her room and had invented an imaginary friend, a little boy who liked to play hide and seek and loved horses as much as she did. Kaylie was worried about her but finally decided that CeCe was simply lonely. When this ordeal ended, she'd enroll CeCe in a kindergarten so she could make some real friends.

Kaylie washed all the bedding in the house, cleaned the

braided rugs and scrubbed the bathrooms until the porcelain shown. In the attic, she found a trunk filled with linens for the mahogany dining table and washed them, then set the table using the Battenberg lace and a set of rose china tucked away in an old chest.

She was ecstatic to find that the sewing machine in the attic worked, so she quilted placemats from scraps of red and green fabric. CeCe needed a project, so they made a Christmas tree for the table using Styrofoam balls they found in the attic, decorating the balls with paint, glitter, buttons, and rickrack.

Although they worked in the mornings, they took the afternoons to play. A picnic by the creek led to wading. Even though the water was chilly, CeCe splashed and jumped up and down with excitement.

They collected small stones that had turned smooth from the water and painted them red and green, then crafted a wreath for the front door, adding fresh greenery from the farm and a holly bush growing beside the house.

Mitch had repaired and painted the front porch, so they decorated it with more fresh holly leaves and berries. The craft store had a sale on Christmas cards and wooden ornaments that CeCe could paint herself and decorate with glitter, and they spent hours making those. Kaylie showed CeCe how to cut out the pictures on the holiday cards, then they strung them with red ribbon.

It was the nicest few days Kaylie had had since her husband's death because CeCe was smiling and happy again.

Not that there weren't tense moments. Moments where she

felt as if someone was watching them. Days where she sensed that their reprieve might be running out.

Days where she and Mitch crossed paths, and the tension between them mounted. He started painting in the upstairs, so she and CeCe had shared a bed, alternating rooms while the other room dried. The den took another day, but the kitchen, with its nooks and crannies, took the longest.

He had kept his distance since that first meeting, had steered clear of her and CeCe to the point where she felt as if he was avoiding them.

That distance relieved her, but at the same time, she found herself yearning to have a conversation with him again. To see the tenderness in his expression when he looked at her daughter.

But when he rode up on Horseshoe and saw the porch and front door decorated, his expression turned dark as if he disapproved of the festive decorations.

CeCe bounced up from the porch and waved to him. "Hey, Mr. Mitch. See the bows Mommy and I made."

Mitch glanced at CeCe's hand where she held a string of red bows, his jaw tight. "You weren't kidding about decorating?"

"We gots to so Santa'll know where to find me," CeCe said innocently.

Mitch's fingers tightened around the reins. "You don't plan on going to your own house for Christmas, Kat?"

Kaylie gritted her teeth, a lie forming on her lips. "We sold our house after my husband passed. CeCe and I are traveling for a while until we decide where we want to settle." One thing she'd learned while hiding was to keep as close to the truth as possible.

Get too detailed with the lies, and it was easy to get tangled up in them.

"Have you decided?" he asked gruffly.

Kaylie glanced across the ranch, the memories she'd made her with her daughter tearing at her. She wished she could buy this place for her and CeCe and stay here forever.

But wishing did no good when they might have to pick up and run any second.

MITCH COULDN'T MISS THE longing on Kat's face as she gazed across his ranch. He dismounted, moved by the fact that she appreciated the land. Sally had never looked at the farmhouse or ranch the way Kat and her daughter did.

Sally had hated the isolation, the smell of the barn, the rundown property and furniture she considered country and outdated. She'd wanted a condo in Austin with chrome and glass, and nights at museums with fancy dinners and expensive champagne.

There was no way in hell she would have made placemats from scraps or a Styrofoam tree for the table, or polished and cleaned every inch of the house herself.

She'd hated the antiques that had belonged to his grandmother and suggested they throw everything out, including the sewing machine Kat had been so excited to find.

Kat reminded him of his grandmother who'd doted on kids, liked baking and gardening, and loved working alongside his grandfather on the ranch.

But seeing Kat and CeCe inside the house also made him feel guilty. His son should be sleeping in the bedroom, wading in the creek and riding Horseshoe.

He still hadn't given CeCe a ride, but she asked him every day.

Emotions welled in his throat, and he swallowed hard. He'd played along with Kat's lies for the past few days, but he didn't think he could stand to have her and her daughter in the house on Christmas Day.

Not when Todd should be here hanging his stocking and waking up to Santa.

"I'll work on the downstairs bathroom in the morning," he said, then turned to CeCe. The persistent little kid wasn't going to give up until he gave her that riding lesson. Might as well get it over with. "How about I let you ride Horseshoe tomorrow after lunch?"

"Really?" CeCe held her breath, melting Mitch's heart.

"Really."

"Yippee!" CeCe raced down the porch steps and threw herself at him, wrapping her arms around his legs.

Pain ricocheted through Mitch's heart so deeply that his legs felt weak. But he managed an awkward pat on her back.

When he looked up at Kat, he thought he saw tears glimmering in her eyes. Compassion for her mushroomed inside him.

She and the kid had lost the man they loved. If he understood one thing, it was grief.

But if they were simply moving around in search of a new home, why the fake ID in her bag?

Mitch forced a smile. "That is if your mother says it's okay," he told CeCe.

CeCe tugged at Kat's arm. "It's okay, right, Mommy? Please, please say it's okay."

Kat licked her lips, the sun glinting off her golden blonde hair. Mitch couldn't help but be drawn to her sea blue eyes, eyes that looked torn over what to say as if it had been a long time since she'd had a break and someone had been nice to her.

But that flicker of wariness darkened the mood.

"We'll do it here in the horse pen so you can watch her every minute," Mitch said, sensing he needed to reassure her he had no ill intentions.

Kat gave a small nod, then squeezed CeCe's shoulder. "Yes, honey, that's fine."

"Once you get the hang of handling Horseshoe, maybe we can all take a ride across the ranch," Mitch said. "There's a pond on the west side."

CeCe reached up to pet Horseshoe's head. "Did you hear that, buddy? I get to ride you tomorrow, and Mr. Mitch is gonna show us the pond!"

Kat looked hesitant again, her expression wary. "Thanks for the offer," she said. "We'll see. I still have a lot to do here."

Mitch narrowed his eyes. "What else? You've cleaned everything. The house looks like it's ready to show."

"I thought I'd make some curtains for the room where CeCe's sleeping."

Mitch tensed. He'd stripped the comforter and curtains Sally had put up because Todd had never liked them. He and Sally had argued about his room more than once. Todd wanted a horse theme but Sally had denied him.

Could he allow this stranger in his house to decorate his son's room the way she wanted?

He rubbed his hand over his pocket where he'd put the fingerprint sample he'd taken from the coffee mug Kat had been drinking from that morning. He had to know who she was before things went any further.

He forced himself to back away. He'd take the print to the lab and find out the truth.

Already the little girl was hacking at his shattered heart. And her mother's vulnerable expression roused protective instincts he had no business feeling for a woman who was lying to him.

For a woman who might be a criminal.

Kaylie watched Mitch ride away, willing her heart to stop fluttering. What was wrong with her?

She had loved her husband dearly. He was the only man she'd ever been with.

But this big, tough cowboy aroused feelings inside her that she hadn't felt in a long time. A longing and sexual need that had been missing from her life.

Truth be told, Joe had lost interest in lovemaking the last two years of their marriage. He'd been preoccupied with business and had shut down emotionally, creating a chasm that she hadn't been able to breach.

Guilt swamped her for even thinking about this stranger

when Joe had been murdered.

"Mommy, I get to ride Horseshoe!" CeCe danced across the grass, skipping and twirling. "I get to ride Horseshoe!"

Kat smiled, grateful Mitch had agreed to give her daughter a riding lesson, but vowing not to let herself even dream about a friendship with the sexy man. There was no use getting attached to him when nothing could come of it but heartache

When getting attached to him might endanger his life.

MITCH RODE HORSESHOE BACK to the stable, unsaddled and brushed him down and put him in the barn to rest for the next day. Weary, he climbed in his SUV and drove to the crime lab.

A half hour later, he poked his head into the office of his friend Sergeant Jonas Walker.

Jonas's eyes shot up. "Mitch? This is a surprise."

Mitch gritted his teeth. His friends had tried to reach out after his wife's and son's deaths, but he'd literally shoved them away with a fist.

Jonas stood and extended his hand. "Sorry, man. I should have said it's good to see you back."

"I'm not back," Mitch said. Not officially anyway.

"But you're sober," Jonas said.

Leave it to his friend to call it like it was. "Yeah, today I am."

"One day at a time," Jonas said, and Mitch remembered that Jonas had struggled with his own issues at one time.

Mitch shifted, struggling over out how to apologize for the

way he'd treated him.

"So, what brings you to the lab?" Jonas asked, smoothing over the awkward moment.

Mitch silently thanked him for not pushing for an apology. But one day Mitch would apologize. He owed that much to his friend.

He removed the evidence bag from his pocket. "I have a print I want you to run."

Jonas narrowed his eyes as he took the bag. "Whose is it?"

"That's what I want you to tell me."

Jonas laid the bag on his desk, then folded his arms. "What's going on, man? I didn't know you were working a case."

"I'm not," he said. "But . . . I'd rather not explain. Can you do me a favor and just run it?"

"Sure," Jonas said. "Not even a hint?"

Mitch jammed his hands in his pockets. "A woman showed up out at my ranch. I think she's in trouble."

"The law after her?"

"I don't know." Mitch hoped not. "But something's off about her. I found fake ID in her suitcase."

"You searched her belongings?" Jonas asked.

"I had my reasons."

"You don't trust anyone, do you, Mitch?"

Mitch shook his head. Not after he'd lost his family. "No."

Jonas frowned. "Just be careful, Mitch."

Mitch had a bad feeling it was too late for that. That he'd already dug himself in too deep. That no matter what he found out, he would still protect Kat and her daughter.

AFTER DINNER, KAYLIE DECIDED she and CeCe needed a grocery run. All afternoon, CeCe had begged her to make Christmas cookies, a tradition Kaylie's mother had started with her when she was young, one she was determined to pass onto her daughter.

Family traditions meant everything to her. Especially when she had no family left. None except the little girl she wanted to see happy again.

She loaded CeCe into the Pathfinder and drove into Twin Branches, but her old habit of checking over her shoulder kicked in, and she couldn't relax.

CeCe chattered about what kind of sprinkles and cookie cutters she wanted and suggested baking a special batch for Mr. Mitch as a present.

CeCe patted the tattered cowboy hat Kaylie had found in the attic and jammed it on her head. "Don't I look like a cowboy, Mommy?"

"A cowgirl," Kaylie said with a grin.

CeCe pushed the other Stetson into Kaylie's hands, and she set it on her head. The hats weren't much in the way of a disguise, but they were big enough to shade her face. And with CeCe in jeans and a plaid shirt and her ponytail tucked under her hat, she could have passed for a boy.

She held her daughter's hand, again scanning the parking lot as they ducked into the grocery store, grabbed a cart and loaded it with supplies. "I want green trees," CeCe said. "And silver bells, and peppermint candy canes."

Kaylie pointed out the box of food coloring and CeCe dropped it into the cart.

"And these!" CeCe grabbed a bottle of sprinkles and tossed them in, along with a pack of Christmas cookie cutters.

"I think we have it," Kaylie said.

"We need milk to go with the cookies," CeCe said.

"True," Kaylie added a gallon of milk to the cart. But the hair on the back of her neck prickled at the sound of a man's voice.

She turned and glanced down the aisle, but a shadow darted away.

Suddenly trembling, she hurried CeCe to the checkout counter, quickly piling their items on top for the cashier to ring up.

"Looks like somebody's making treats for Santa," the chubby middle-aged woman manning the register said.

"Me and Mommy are making 'em for Mr. Mitch."

The woman peered over her glasses. "Mr. Mitch?"

"Yeah," CeCe said. "He's teaching me to ride Horseshoe."

"CeCe, don't bother the woman," Kaylie said, anxious to leave the store.

"No bother, honey," the woman said. "Are y'all new in town?"

Kaylie's lungs squeezed for air. She felt that odd tingling again as if someone was watching her, breathing down her neck.

"We're just passing through," Kaylie said. CeCe started to speak up, but Kaylie squeezed her hand so tightly her daughter looked up at her, her smile wilting.

"Come on, sweet pea," she said as she gave the woman some cash.

The woman's expression turned to worry as if she sensed something was wrong. But Kaylie didn't bother to explain.

She rushed CeCe out to the Pathfinder, threw the groceries in the back, and peeled from the parking lot.

She held her breath until they turned the corner outside of town, then released a relieved sigh when she thought she'd escaped.

A second later, headlights nearly blinded her, and a car raced up on her tail. She clenched the steering wheel in a white-knuckled grip, praying she was wrong about the car following her.

Speeding up, she glanced at CeCe, guilt dogging her for the fear in her little girl's eyes.

The excitement of the cookie making and riding lesson was lost as the car slammed into them and sent the Pathfinder careening toward a ditch.

CHAPTER 7

Mitch made a last minute decision to wait while Jonas ran the fingerprint. If Kat was a criminal, he needed to know.

Although for the life of him, he couldn't imagine the homebody he'd seen sewing placemats and stringing holly with her daughter ever having done anything wrong.

But he'd been fooled before.

And paid the price.

Jonas plugged the print into the computer, and they watched as the computer system made comparisons through all the major databases.

"Where did you say you lifted the print?" Jonas asked, still fishing.

Mitch cleared his throat. "Off a coffee mug in my house."

Jonas jerked his head toward Mitch. "Did the woman buy the ranch?"

He'd told Jonas his plans to sell one night when he'd been drowning his sorrow. "No, but I put an ad in the local paper."

"She made an offer?"

"Not exactly." Mitch wiped a drop of perspiration from his forehead. "She moved in though and made herself at home in the farmhouse."

"You mean she broke in?"

Mitch shrugged. "Yeah."

"Does she know who you are? That you own it?"

Mitch shook his head. "She looked nervous, so I told her I was a handyman fixing up the place. She claimed she was a real estate agent, said places sold better if they were furnished so she's been cleaning like the devil and decorating it for Christmas."

Jonas looked concerned. "So she's squatting, and you think she's in trouble?"

Mitch nodded. "That about sizes it up."

The computer program kept running but came up with no match.

"She's not in the system," Jonas said. "That's a good sign."

"Yeah." But he had seen fear in her eyes. And she did have those fake IDs.

"Maybe she's running from an ex."

"Could be. She said her husband was dead."

"She could be lying."

"I know. Except her little girl said her daddy was in heaven, so I think that part may be true."

"Jesus, Mitch. You didn't say she had a kid."

Mitch's heart gave a pang. "Hell, Jonas, that's the only reason I didn't throw her out." That and he was intrigued by her.

Attracted to her, too.

But that was a problem he didn't want to share with Jonas.

He tucked his hat back on his head, then thanked Jonas and strode out the door. The ride back to his ranch made him strengthen his resolve to stay on guard.

Once he crossed through Twin Branches and turned onto the road leading back to the ranch, anxiety needled him.

When he rounded the bend, he saw Kat's Pathfinder on the side of the road in the ditch, and fear seized his chest.

Had something bad happened to Kat and CeCe?

KAYLIE HUGGED CECE TO her, rocking her back and forth. Her daughter had been terrified and screaming when the SUV had ground to a stop. "Shh, it's okay, baby, we're all right."

"But you screamed," CeCe whispered. "And I was scared, Mommy."

"I know and I'm sorry," Kaylie said, wishing she could shield her daughter from everything bad in life.

But she hadn't. She and Joe had both failed.

Thankfully the car that had hit them had zoomed on past. For a horrifying second, she'd thought he was going to whip around and hit her again, but a truck had driven by, and if the driver of the car had intended to come back, he changed his mind.

Headlights lit the road, the sound of another truck rumbling to a halt making her stiffen. She glanced back and saw the lights dim, then flicker off, and recognized Mitch's black pickup truck.

Nerves gathered in her stomach. She'd hoped to get them out of the ditch and back to the ranch without Mitch being aware of her accident. But he parked and strode toward her, that confident cowboy swagger sending a mixture of relief and trepidation through her.

"Mommy?" CeCe sniffled.

"It's okay, honey. Mr. Mitch is here."

CeCe relaxed in her arms and wiped at her eyes. "He'll take care of us, won't he, Mommy?"

Kaylie didn't know how to respond. She'd once trusted Joe to take care of them, and he'd been murdered in their house. Then she'd trusted the police, but Arnold and Rafferty had both been shot on the job.

Now she had no one to depend on but herself.

Mitch rapped on the window and opened her car door, and Kaylie braced herself.

"Kat, are you and CeCe okay?"

The tenderness and worry in his deep, gruff voice tore at her composure, and she gulped back a sob.

He cupped her face in his hands to examine her, then lifted CeCe's chin. "Are you hurt, Kat? Sweetpea?"

"We're fine," Kaylie said.

"I was scared," CeCe cried. "And Mommy screamed real loud."

Kaylie blinked back tears, but Mitch must have seen them because he stooped down beside them and pulled them both into his arms.

Kaylie collapsed against him, savoring the feel of his comforting embrace. She gave herself a few minutes to stop shaking, then summoned her courage.

Mitch thumbed her hair away from her face as he searched her eyes. "What happened?"

"It was just an accident," Kaylie said in a low voice.

"This car hitted us!" CeCe cried. "He made us runned off the road."

Anger slashed Mitch's features. "Is that true, Kat?"

She wanted to lie. To take CeCe and run.

But Christmas was two days away, and CeCe had been happier the last week than she had in months.

Poor CeCe had lost so much already.

Didn't her daughter deserve to at least have Santa visit before they had to run again?

MITCH HELD KAT AND her daughter until they both stopped trembling. When Kat pulled away, her face was flushed, her breathing erratic.

"Did you see the car that hit you?" Mitch asked.

She shook her head. "No, the lights blinded me."

Mitch reached for his phone. "We should report this to the sheriff."

Panic flared in Kat's eyes. "No, no sheriff."

Suspicions rose in his mind. "Why not? This was a hit and run."

"I'm sure it was an accident," Kat said. "Besides, I told you I didn't see the vehicle or driver." She pressed a hand to her daughter's cheek. "And we're okay, aren't we, CeCe?"

CeCe nodded, although her expression indicated that she wasn't okay at all. She was terrified.

"Then I'll call a tow truck."

Kat shook her head again. "Let's just see if we can get my SUV out of the ditch. I think it's still drivable."

Mitch hesitated. He wished to hell Kat would tell him the truth about what was going on, but she seemed hell-bent on clinging to her secrets. Maybe her husband really wasn't dead. She could have kidnapped her daughter to escape him and simply told CeCe that he'd gone to heaven.

"All right. You and CeCe sit in my truck, and I'll see what I can do."

Mitch waited until they were tucked safely inside his pickup, then cranked the engine to the SUV. It took him fifteen minutes of maneuvering to extract the Pathfinder from the ditch, but Kat was right, the vehicle was drivable and hadn't sustained any serious damage. A dent in the front fender, but that was it.

He parked in front of his truck, climbed out and met her as she and CeCe jumped from his truck.

"Thank you, Mitch."

His gaze met hers, but she averted her eyes. "You're welcome.

I'll follow you back to the ranch."

CeCe tugged on Mitch's hand. "Can I ride in your truck?"

"Sure, if your mom says it's okay."

Kat frowned. "Not tonight, baby. I want you to keep Mommy company."

CeCe started to protest, but Kat ushered her toward the car. "If you want to make those cookies, do as Mommy says."

That quieted CeCe, and she crawled in the back seat of the Pathfinder and hugged her rag doll to her chest.

Mitch went to his truck and followed them home, his gut instincts warning him that tonight's accident had shaken up Kat more than she wanted to admit.

That she might run.

But the thought of these two vulnerable females on their own with an attacker after them made his blood boil.

No way in hell he'd let them go.

Her fingerprints might not have been in the system, but he'd lift one of those fake IDs and run her picture through the DMV.

Then he'd learn who she really was and why she was squatting in his house.

KAYLIE TUCKED CECE INTO bed, her pulse still unsteady from the accident. What if CeCe had been hurt in the crash?

She couldn't lose her daughter.

"Mommy, can I still ride Horseshoe tomorrow?" CeCe asked.

The resilience of children amazed her. Of course, Mitch's presence had comforted both of them.

She couldn't get used to it.

"Yes, sweetie." But as soon as Christmas was over, they had to move on.

And do what? Keep running forever?

No, just until Buckham was caught.

"Now, get some sleep, honey." Kaylie brushed her daughter's hair from her cheek. "Tomorrow we'll make curtains for this room, then bake cookies."

"And ride with Mr. Mitch?"

Kaylie released a tired breath. "Yes, and ride with Mr. Mitch."

She kissed her daughter's forehead, slipped from the room and closed the door. She'd hoped Mitch was gone, but he was waiting downstairs in the kitchen.

His eyes darkened as she entered. "Is she really okay?"

Kaylie nodded. "She's so excited about her riding lesson tomorrow that she's already forgotten about the accident."

"How about you?" Mitch asked.

A shiver rippled up Kaylie's spine. "I'm fine. Thanks for helping us tonight."

A muscle ticked in Mitch's cheek. "No problem. Why don't you tell me what's going on, Kat, and I'll do even more."

Kaylie tensed. She'd listened to the radio on the way back to the ranch, hoping to hear that Buckham was back in jail, but the news reporter said the manhunt was still underway.

They were also still looking for her for questioning about Joe's death.

Mitch lifted her chin with his thumb. "Kat, talk to me."

"Nothing's going on, Mitch. Just let it go."

Mitch took her hands in his and forced her to look at him. "You're scared of something. I see it in your eyes."

"Mitch, please—"

"You can trust me, Kat. Talk to me."

Kaylie ached to do just that. She'd been on her own too long, running from Buckham and now whoever was working with him.

But Arnold and Rafferty were murdered, and until she knew who'd killed them, she couldn't trust anyone.

Besides, trusting Mitch would make him a target.

"I'm tired, Mitch. Please just go." And don't ask any more of me.

Not when she was so close to the breaking point that she felt herself shattering from the inside out.

"Kat, I want to help." His voice cracked. "Please let me."

"You did help," she said, her resolve strengthening.

His fingers softened around her arms, his gaze latching with hers. She was suddenly drowning in his bedroom eyes. Seduced into safety by his touch.

Then he lowered his head and pressed his lips against hers, and she lost herself in his kiss.

CeCe curled up with her doll and closed her eyes, but she kept seeing that ditch coming for her and her mommy, and she wanted to scream again.

She bit her tongue though. She didn't want to scare her mommy. And she didn't want Mr. Mitch to think she was a big fat crybaby.

She wasn't no crybaby, but she was scared whoever hitted her and Mommy would come back and hit them again, or shoot them like that bad man shot her daddy.

Her stomach hurt, and she opened her eyes and looked up at the window. The moon glowed like a big orange ball through the window.

Maybe Mommy would make those curtains tomorrow so the moon couldn't see inside. So nobody could.

Cause if the bad man looked through the window, he'd find her, and then she'd be bloody and dead like daddy.

Tears pushed at her eyes. She missed her daddy somethin' awful.

'Cept she liked Mr. Mitch and that made her feel good and bad at the same time. It felt good when he wrapped his big arms around her and Mommy like nothing could hurt them as long as Mr. Mitch held them.

But she shouldn't like him so much, not when he wasn't her daddy. Would Daddy be mad that she liked Mr. Mitch?

She liked his horsie and the ranch here, and she liked Todd. He was her new best friend. He told her secrets about the rocks he and his daddy used to pick out of the creek. He showed her some special toys under the bed and said she could play with them. There were farm animals and a stable and horses.

She didn't want to leave. But on the way home Mommy said they'd have to after Santa Claus came.

She wanted Santa to bring her that kitty cat so bad. And maybe a horsie like Horseshoe.

And maybe even a new daddy like Mr. Mitch . . .

She missed her own one 'cept there were things she hadn't told her mommy, like about the big, fat mean man who came to see her daddy when her mommy was out buying chicken to fry one day, and the time she heard her daddy cussing on the phone with someone.

Then he'd strung that key on a ribbon and made a necklace for her dollie with it and said she had to keep the key safe for him. He'd hidden some money in a bag and made her promise not to tell or else he'd give her a spanking.

She wondered if Mr. Mitch kept secrets or if he'd spank his little girl if he had one.

CHAPTER 8

Mitch deepened the kiss, his body humming to life as if it had been asleep for decades.

Kat tasted sweet and delicious, and he sensed a hunger inside her that rivaled his own.

Except she had just been shaken by an accident, and he was taking advantage of her vulnerability.

Still, he liked the way she felt in his arms. The soft purr of her breath as she leaned into him. The way her body fit against his.

The feminine scent that heated his blood and reminded him that he was alive.Guilt slammed into him. How could he enjoy kissing another woman, taking pleasure from her, when his wife and son had died because of him?

He pulled away, his breath heaving out as he released Kat. "I'm sorry. I shouldn't have done that."

Kat looked just as stricken as he felt. "Just go, Mitch. Please go."

The quiver in her voice alarmed him. Was she afraid of him physically?

Or afraid of what she felt? Because she had felt the heat between them just as he had. That was obvious from the way she'd dug her fingers into his back and pulled him closer.

"Kat?"

"Please, Mitch. I need to check on CeCe."

He gave a clipped nod and let her go, although he realized she was making an excuse to put some distance between them.

That was fine. He needed distance himself.

She disappeared up the steps, and he turned to leave. But the sight of the clean house with the placemats and decorations caught him off guard again.

Kat had turned the farmhouse into a *home*. Not just a house, but it felt warm and inviting. For a brief second, he saw Todd racing through the hallway chasing CeCe and laughing.

Pain seared him, and he threw open the front door and rushed outside. He leaned over the porch rail, gulping in a breath to relieve the nausea building inside him as he looked across the ranch.

Moonlight streaked the horizon, a cool breeze stirring the trees and tossing dried leaves across the land. Maybe he'd visit Jack Daniels tonight.

Distract himself from thinking about the gorgeous blonde who was turning him inside out with her sweet smile and home-making, and her cherub daughter who laughed like an angel.

Even more disturbing, he sensed neither of them had laughed for a while just as he hadn't.

In the distance, headlights flickered along the dusty road leading to the ranch.

Mitch squared his shoulders and focused on the vehicle. It slowed as if it might turn, then went on, but the hairs on the back of his neck prickled.

No Jack for him tonight. He had to remain alert.

Was the driver looking for something? Could he have been the one who'd hit Kat and driven her and CeCe off the road?

If he was, what did he want?

———

KAYLIE WAS SO SHAKEN by the kiss she locked herself in the bedroom, slipped on her pjs, turned on the television and crawled in bed. A horror movie was playing so she switched channels and stumbled on the news.

"There is still a manhunt underway for Larry Buckham, a man convicted of murdering Joe Whittaker and two other families in Texas. Although Buckham was convicted, his attorney has filed an appeal citing new evidence that proves he is not the serial killer, the Family Man."

The reporter turned to a woman dressed in a designer suit with lacquered red hair and square glasses. "Buckham's attorney, Willa Barnaby, is here to discuss the case."

"I regret that my client Larry Buckham escaped from prison when we were so close to his appeal being granted and his case being reexamined. Although Joe Whittaker's wife testified against Mr. Buckham, the DA made a strong case that painted him as being the serial murderer who gunned down several families in their homes. This implication swayed the jury to convict him, and strongly influenced the judge's decision in sentencing. However, the prosecutor supplied no concrete evidence to link Buckham to the other crimes. Based on that fact, I'm requesting a new investigation and Mr. Buckham's case to be reopened.

"This morning, I spoke with police who confirm that they are looking into Mr. Whittaker's finances and the fact that he might have been laundering money. With that information at hand, investigators may focus on enemies Whittaker made through his business."

The newscaster held up a finger. "I'm sorry to interrupt you, Ms. Barnaby, but news has just come in regarding the murder of another Texas family."

Kaylie sat up straighter, glued to the television. First of all, she knew Larry Buckham had killed Joe. She *had* heard his gravelly voice.

Hadn't she?

And what was that business about Joe laundering money? Joe would never . . .

Snippets of conversations spoken in hushed voices, of late-night phone calls, of weekend business trips, taunted her, and a cold chill engulfed her.

Had Joe somehow gotten himself in trouble?

"This late breaking story in," the reporter said as the camera focused on the outside of a Texas stucco home in a small town called Bend Creek. "A woman, man, and their two teenage sons were murdered in their home tonight. Neighbors reported hearing a commotion at the house a half hour ago, and someone called 911. By the time the police arrived, the family was dead, the killer gone."

The camera showed the police surrounding the house, blue lights swirling, officers combing the property.

"While police can't confirm that the killer is the same man who murdered the other families, they have admitted that the MO is the same. If you have any information regarding this crime, please call the police."

Kaylie worried her lower lip with her teeth. First, Buckham's lawyer was trying to convince people he was innocent.

But no other families had been murdered while he was in prison suggesting he was guilty.

But now he was on the loose, another family had died. A family from Bend Creek. Bend Creek was only twenty miles from Twin Branches.

She clenched the sheets with clammy hands.

Had Buckham killed them? And if so, why Bend Creek? Was he trying to let her know that he was close by? That he knew where she was hiding?

She slid off the bed and paced the room, then checked out the window. The ranch looked quiet. Serene.

But she felt anything but peaceful.

She was tempted to call Mitch and ask him to stay the night.

And kiss her again.

But that would be stupid and dangerous.

For CeCe's sake, she had to play it smart and not allow her emotions to rule her decisions.

The reporter's comment about Joe and money laundering hacked at her conscience. Joe had handled other people's money, wealthy people.

When he first died, the police had searched his files looking for motive and found nothing.

But Buckham's lawyer suggested otherwise.

The detective had asked questions about Joe's clients, but she hadn't been able to tell them much. Joe rarely shared information about work because he respected his client's confidentiality.

He hadn't made a fortune, but he'd managed their money pretty well, and they'd been comfortable. Although one of the officers who'd questioned her had mentioned some discrepancies in Joe's accounting.

Dammit, she wished she had a computer so she could review all their past bank statements and Joe's portfolio. But the police had confiscated that, and for her own safety, she'd been warned about touching their accounts or contacting anyone associated with Joe. A killer could track her if she left a paper trail.

But the cash she had was running out. If Buckham wasn't found soon, she didn't know what she'd do.

She opened the envelope that she'd found hidden in the back of one of Joe's gym bags when she'd packed up his clothes for Goodwill. At the last minute, she'd tucked it inside the overnight bag she kept for a quick getaway, deciding she might need the information about the accounts at some point. But she'd forgotten about it during the stressful months. She'd been too busy running and trying to appease her daughter.

Hoping to find something to clear Joe, she skimmed through the paperwork, looking for anything her husband might have hidden from her. The normal bills and deposits from clients, although about six months before he died she noticed a definite spike in their income.

Income that he'd deposited into a separate account.

Why had he hidden it from her? Was he building a nest egg for their retirement or for a trip to surprise her?

Or . . . what if the police were right? Joe had acted strange, distant, worried the last few months.

Had Joe crossed the line and skimmed money from a client, or accepted payment for illegal business activities?

And if he'd hidden money from her, what else had he been hiding?

MITCH PACED THE CABIN all night, unable to sleep. The tortured emotions the kiss stirred in him made him want to run from Kat. But she and CeCe needed help.

And he had never walked away from a woman or child in need.

He kept vigil from his porch till dawn, looking for that vehicle to reappear and watching for trouble. But only the quiet of the ranch and the night sounds surrounded him.

Finally, he showered, had coffee and slipped back into the

farmhouse. Kat was in the shower so he eased into her room and found the fake IDs in her bag. He lifted one of the driver licenses, then tiptoed down the steps, hurrying when he heard the shower water kick off.

Dammit, he'd like to join her in there. He envisioned the silhouette of her sexy, naked body beneath the warm spray of water with soap bubbles beading on her golden skin.

Frustrated at the effect the images had on his body, he plowed out the front door but paused to close it quietly. The last thing he wanted was for Kat to know he was snooping around, investigating her.

He crossed the grass to his cabin on the hill, climbed in his truck and drove toward the Ranger office. He bypassed his boss's office, not ready to be back at work.

His buddy Micah Hardin loped in wearing a shit-eating grin. A few weeks ago, he'd helped Micah catch one of the prison escapees who'd stalked a woman named Lenora Lockhart. Apparently, Micah was in love with Lenora now.

"Good to see you here at work, Mitch."

Mitch made a harrumph sound. "I'm not. I just needed to use one of the computers."

Micah arched a brow. "What's going on?"

Mitch had already told Jonas more than he'd meant to. But he and Micah had been partners, and if he could trust anyone, it was Micah.

He motioned for Micah to follow him, and they ducked into the office they shared. "I need to run a photo ID through the DMV records."

"Whose ID?"

Mitch quickly explained about the situation with Kat, although he omitted the part about her turning his farmhouse into a cozy home, and that he'd kissed her.

"Let me see it." Micah studied the photo. "Her hair looks dyed in this picture. It's an unnatural black."

"Yeah, she's a blonde now. I know it's a fake ID," Mitch said. "She had a couple of others in her bag."

Mitch scanned the photo and watched the computer program run. Five minutes later, a positive ID popped up.

"Kaylie Whittaker, age 29, home address Austin."

"Shit," Micah said. "I thought her face looked familiar."

"What do you mean?"

"You obviously haven't watched the news."

No, he hadn't. He'd been too busy feeling sorry for himself, drowning his sorrows in booze. "I guess I dropped off the earth for a while." He gestured toward the photo. "So what do you know?"

"Kaylie Whittaker's husband Joe, a financial planner in Austin, was murdered in her home one night."

"By the serial Family Man killer?"

"That's what the police thought. Although the killer wore a mask, Kaylie Whittaker identified the man as Larry Buckham and testified against him."

Dread surged through Mitch. "He escaped in the prison break, didn't he?"

Micah nodded. "The only one who hasn't been caught yet."

"Dammit, that's why she's running scared."

"There's more," Micah said. "Apparently Buckham's lawyer has been working on an appeal and claims that Buckham is not the Family Man killer, that the two cases aren't related. That Joe Whittaker was laundering money and his illegal activities might have had something to do with his death. His wife is wanted for questioning."

Sweat beaded on Mitch's neck. "They think she killed her husband?"

"The theory is that she discovered his illegal business affairs, shot him, then pinned the blame on Buckham."

"I don't believe it," Mitch said. "She's not a killer."

Micah narrowed his eyes. "You know her that well?"

Yes. No. She'd lied to him.

But images of her sewing those damn placemats and braiding CeCe's hair, and making homemade chicken and dumplings, in his kitchen taunted him. "I've seen her with her little girl. She's not a killer."

"Jesus, Mitch, if she's at your place, you need to turn her over to the sheriff and let them sort this out. If she's innocent, they'll get to the truth."

But in the meantime, CeCe would be taken away from her mother, placed in foster care, have to listen to accusations about her mother killing her father. The investigation might take months.

And sometimes the system failed.

"Although there's one thing working in her favor," Micah said.

"What's that?"

"Last night the Family Man killer struck again. He killed a man, woman and their two teenage sons in Bend Creek."

Mitch swallowed hard. Bend Creek. Jesus, that was close to Twin Branches. "So Buckham could be the serial killer?"

Micah shrugged. "Could be."

Although if Buckham was the serial killer and his lawyer was about to get his sentence overturned and a new trial, breaking out of prison and killing another family was stupid on his part.

Of course, most of the criminals Mitch had met weren't exactly genius material.

Kat's—no, Kaylie's—accident the night before took on a more ominous feeling. Just what kind of evidence did Buckham's attorney have against Joe Whittaker and Kaylie?

Was she running from guilt, or because a man was trying to kill her?

CHAPTER 9

KAYLIE CLEANED UP THE BREAKFAST dishes while CeCe drew a *Dear Santa* card at the table.

Her heart squeezed at the picture of a yellow kitten.

"We gots to get a tree," CeCe said. "And stockings for the fireplace."

Kaylie smiled, although guilt nagged at her for using a stranger's home and making it her own. If she could figure out a way to buy the ranch, she would.

But after looking at her finances, that was impossible. And even if she did have the money, they couldn't stay here, not with Larry Buckham hunting for them.

What if he'd been driving the car that hit them the night before?

CeCe colored the kitten yellow. "Can we get a tree today, Mommy?"

"I don't know," Kaylie said, hesitant to make a promise she might not be able to keep.

"But we gots to," CeCe said. "Or Santa won't know where to leave the presents."

Oh, good grief. *Presents.* She'd been so busy worrying about their safety that she hadn't done any shopping. She had nothing to give her daughter. Not a toy or surprise. Nothing.

She couldn't very well go into town and shop either, not and leave her five-year-old alone.

Maybe she could find something in the attic to make CeCe a gift. A new doll or stuffed toy. She'd be disappointed not to find a kitten under the tree, but Kaylie would explain that a kitten would come later.

When they were settled and safe again.

CeCe drew a tree by the kitten and colored balls as decorations, then added a yellow star at the top. "There. Now let's find a real tree."

"Honey, I need to look around in the attic first. Maybe when we take that ride later, we can ask Mitch to show us a good spot to cut down one."

"Yippee!" CeCe shouted. "I can't wait to ride Horseshoe."

Emotions welled in Kaylie's throat as they climbed the steps to the attic, and she flipped on the light. The trunk she'd pulled the fabric scraps from had been a treasure trove. A second trunk sat beside it, and she and CeCe opened it and rummaged through the contents.

"Look, Mommy." CeCe pulled a toy pony from a box. "He looks like Horseshoe."

Kaylie smiled as CeCe began bouncing the toy across the floor as if it was galloping in the pasture. Beneath a box of costume jewelry, she found an old worn quilt, a nine patch made with squares of horses appliqued on each square. CeCe might like some of the jewelry, but she had no right to take anything from this house, so she put the box back in place.

"Look, CeCe, isn't this quilt beautiful?" Kaylie unfolded it, admiring the delicate handmade stitches. "I wonder who made it."

CeCe ran over to trace her finger over the outline of a black stallion. "Can we put it on my bed?"

Kaylie hesitated. What would the owner of the ranch think if he knew she'd been plundering through his belongings? If he saw what she'd done in his house?

He wouldn't, she silently vowed. He'd hired Mitch to paint the inside to fix it up to sell. She'd pack up all the things she'd used before she and CeCe left.

"I guess that would be all right," Kaylie said. "But I'm going to wash it first. It's been packed up for a while." She'd hand wash it to preserve the handwork.

She spied other fabric in the bottom of the trunk as well and decided she could make new doll clothes for CeCe's doll and fashion a baby carriage and blanket from the scraps.

Satisfied, she carried the quilt down the steps while CeCe took the pony to her room. Kaylie hand washed the quilt and put it in the dryer on low, then found CeCe lying on her belly in the bedroom playing.

"Look, Mommy," CeCe said. "My friend showed me the toys under the bed."

"Your friend?"

CeCe nodded. "I told you about him. Todd. He loves the ponies best."

Kaylie worried her bottom lip with her teeth, wondering if she should comment on CeCe's imaginary friend but decided to play along with her for now.

So she simply smiled as CeCe arranged the small toy ponies around the stable, then added the farm animals and horses, setting them around as if they were grazing in the pasture.

The owner of the ranch must have had children. Why had he left the toys behind?

* * *

MITCH STEWED OVER THE situation with Kat—no, Kaylie— and her daughter as he drove back to the ranch.

He had done more research on the Whittakers and discovered that Kaylie did indeed work as a real estate agent and her daughter's name was CeCe.

But she'd omitted the part about being wanted for questioning as a suspect in her husband's murder.

She had also been in protective custody under an officer named Arnold Pinter, but he'd been found shot to death the night she disappeared.

One report suggested that she'd killed the man because she felt like Buckham's attorney was going to clear him and prove that she murdered her husband.

But the other scenario, which sounded more reasonable after

having met her, was that Buckham or someone working for him had found the safe house, had shot Kaylie's guard, so she'd fled to save herself and CeCe.

By the time he reached the ranch, he was ready to confront her.

But when he saw Kaylie and CeCe decorating Christmas cookies, his heart tugged, and he put the questions on hold.

He'd wait until they were alone to discuss the situation. No sense upsetting the sweet little girl. Besides, Christmas music played in the background, and CeCe was humming *Here Comes Santa Claus* as she spread icing on the cookies.

"Look, Mr. Mitch, I made trees and a stocking and a star," CeCe said. "And we made teddy bears and ornament cookies, too!"

"I see." He couldn't resist. He wiped a dollop of icing from her cheek and licked his finger. "Yum."

CeCe giggled and shook the sprinkles over the ornament cookies. "I made Santa a card today to tell him about the kitty cat I want."

"You want a kitten?"

"Yep, an orange one," CeCe said. "Kitties like to live on ranches, don't they?"

"Yes, they do," Mitch said his gut tightening. Did Kaylie really plan on staying?

She had to realize that her lies would be revealed sooner or later, that the owner would eventually show up.

How would she react when she learned he was that owner?

"Does Santa have kitty cats at the North Pole?" CeCe asked.

Kaylie's gaze met his, a small smile curving her mouth. She had icing on her nose and fingers, too, and white powdered sugar dotted her shirt. The two of them looked adorable and so vulnerable that he immediately dismissed the idea that Kaylie could have shot her husband or been involved in anything illegal.

Foolish to judge her based on emotions, but the little girl's holiday spirit was contagious.

"I think Santa has kitties for special little girls," Mitch said.

"I'm special," CeCe said as she placed two raisins on the bear cookies for eyes. "My mommy says so. And my daddy said so, too."

"I'm sure he thought you were very special," Mitch said, wishing he knew more about the man who'd married Kaylie.

And about his killer.

Maybe he should talk to Buckham's lawyer and find out exactly what evidence she had that would exonerate Buckham from the crime.

And if Buckham hadn't killed Joe Whittaker, who had?

———————

KAYLIE HAD NO IDEA what she was going to do about the kitten.

Or about Mitch.

He was starting to get under her skin in a serious way. The fact that he was so kind and gentle with CeCe only intensified the draw she felt toward him.

She stood by the horse pen and watched as he showed CeCe

how to mount Horseshoe. "He's the tamest horse I've ever worked with," Mitch said.

"He does seem like he's good with kids," Kaylie said.

That pained look darkened his eyes for a second, then he gave a short nod. "He is." He turned back to CeCe. "Like I told you before, sweet pea, animals sense when people like them. You have to be kind to him, but also show him you're in control."

He showed her how to use the reins to guide Horseshoe, and how to nudge him gently with her feet as she gave him commands. "When you want him to slow down or stop, pull back on the reins so he feels pressure against his neck and say, 'whoa.'"

CeCe giggled and patted the horse's neck. "I luvs you, Horseshoe."

Kaylie's heart swelled with love at the smile on her daughter's face. The past few months had been hell, but she was thankful for the brief reprieve they'd enjoyed these last few days.

CeCe would have her Christmas and Santa if it was the last thing she ever did.

Then she'd find someone to help them out of this mess and protect them from Larry Buckham.

Running was no way for her child to live.

"Let's practice around the stable first," Mitch said. "Then maybe we'll saddle a horse for your mother and ride out to the pond."

"Can we pick a Christmas tree?" CeCe asked.

Kaylie held her breath, hoping Mitch would agree. If not, she and CeCe would go hiking and find one themselves.

"Sure," Mitch said. "You can pick it out, CeCe."

Her daughter beamed with joy at the idea. The temperature had fallen near freezing the night before but had risen to the fifties now. The wind tossed Kaylie's hair around her face, and she tied it back with a scarf as Mitch led Horseshoe around the inside of the pen.

Her daughter was a natural and, within minutes, had taken charge of the animal. Mitch was right—Horseshoe was gentle and followed CeCe's commands as if he'd lived with a child on his back.

"Do you know how to ride, Kat?"

"Yes," she said. "I worked on a horse farm during the summers during high school."

"Good. I'll saddle horses for us so we can ride out to the pond."

She nodded, opened the gate and stepped into the pen, then walked over and petted Horseshoe.

"You're doing great up there, CeCe."

CeCe formed a little pout with her mouth. "I wish he was mine."

Kaylie wished that, too. Unfortunately, wishes didn't always come true.

MITCH KEPT HIS EYES peeled for trouble as they rode across his pasture. It was too chilly to wade in the edge of the creek, but he taught CeCe how to skip rocks at the pond, his heart hammering as he remembered how excited Todd had been when they'd done the same thing.

God, he wished his son was here now.

In spite of the constant ache in his chest, he couldn't help but smile at the pure pleasure on the little girl's face.

Her mother's smile as she relaxed was breathtaking as well.

Dragging his gaze from her, Mitch helped CeCe mount Horseshoe again, and the three of them rode across the pasture toward the woods.

"The ranchland is so beautiful," Kaylie said as they slowed the horses by a wooded section. "I wonder why the owner is selling."

Because the ranch held all his dreams and those died when he buried his boy.

Instead of admitting the heartfelt truth, his throat closed with emotions, making it impossible to speak, so he simply shrugged.

"Are we gettin' a tree now?" CeCe asked, drawing him back to the task at hand.

Mitch slid down from his bay. "Sure. I bet we'll find the perfect one in the woods."

Kaylie dismounted while he helped CeCe from the saddle. They left the horses to graze, and Mitch grabbed his handsaw and led the way.

CeCe ran from tree to tree, pointing out the tallest and biggest ones she could find.

"Sweetpea, we'd have to cut a hole in the ceiling for that one," Mitch said with a wink.

Kaylie walked over to a six-foot pine. "How about this one. The needles should hold the ornaments we made, CeCe."

CeCe danced around the tree singing *Santa Claus Is Coming to Town* while Mitch sawed the tree down. He dragged it back to the pond where they'd left the horses, then tied it to his saddlebag while CeCe gathered pinecones to make more decorations.

By the time they rode back, the sun was setting. Kaylie helped him unsaddle and brush the horses while CeCe combed Horseshoe's mane. Mitch stowed the animals in the barn while Kaylie walked CeCe to the house to start dinner.

By the time he dragged the tree into the den by the fireplace, the scent of fried chicken wafted from the kitchen. His stomach growled, the memory of his grandmother frying chicken in her cast iron pan making him itch to join Kaylie and CeCe.

But he stepped to the kitchen door to say goodnight and leave them to decorate the tree.

CeCe raced over and grabbed his hand. "Come on, Mr. Mitch, Mommy has dinner all ready!"

The child's exuberance made him wish he could change the fact that her daddy was dead. "You enjoy it. I'll see you two later."

"No way." Kaylie brushed her hands on her jeans and motioned for him to grab a plate. "This is my way of thanking you for the riding lesson and for helping us with the tree."

Mitch's gaze met hers, his emotions churning. She looked more rested than she had when she'd arrived, not frightened as she had after the accident, and her cheeks were pink from the cold.

His mouth watered for the food, but also for a taste of her ripe lips.

Good God. He was crazy. He could not keep flirting with danger when the damn woman was mired deep in horse dung with the law.

He had to keep his eyes peeled in case Buckham showed up at the ranch.

If he tried to hurt Kaylie or CeCe, he'd kill the bastard himself.

GOD DAMMIT, THE STUPID bitch was staying at a ranch owned by a fucking Texas Ranger.

He couldn't believe his shitty luck.

Worse, the cowboy obviously had his dick in a knot over her. He'd been following her around all day like a lovesick dog, playing with the kid, cutting down a sappy Christmas tree. And now they were inside eating dinner, all cozy like they were a family when the bitch should be dead.

She'd made everyone think he'd killed those families. Stupid woman. She had no idea what her husband had been up to.

No idea what he'd had going on the side.

In the end, Joe Whittaker had gotten what he deserved.

Even though he'd wrapped his lawyer around his finger and his boss had paid her to clear him of those family murders, she still hadn't promised he'd be free of the charges against Whittaker.

Not with the man's wife's teary testimony.

The very reason Kaylie had to die.

CHAPTER 10

MITCH DEVOURED THE HOME cooked meal, then built a fire in the fireplace to ward off the chill while Kaylie cleaned up the dishes.

CeCe had chattered nonstop during dinner about decorating the Christmas tree, so he dug out the tree stand from the attic along with a string of lights and set it up in front of the window.

"It's beautiful!" CeCe shouted as the white lights blinked on and off.

Kaylie stood in the doorway, her eyes sparkling with appreciation as if it had been a long time since anyone had done something nice for her.

Now he understood the reason.

"It is gorgeous and it smells so good," Kaylie said. "I've always preferred a real tree."

"Me, too." Mitch swallowed back emotions her words stirred. "It needs some decorations."

"We made some!" CeCe said, bouncing up and down on her little pink sneakers.

Kaylie played a Christmas CD while CeCe led him to a box in the corner holding homemade ornaments crafted from Styrofoam and Christmas cards they'd strung with ribbon. The box reminded him of his grandmother and her crafts.

CeCe carefully removed a snowman ornament and hung it on the tree, singing along with the Christmas music in the background. Mitch folded his arms and watched mother and daughter hang the decorations, his memories of Todd so vivid that he felt as if his son was there.

"We need a star on top," CeCe said when the box had been emptied and the limbs hung heavy with the ornaments.

"I saw one upstairs when I was moving boxes from the storage room." Mitch left the room and retrieved the star he'd packed away after Todd's death. His hand shook as he carried it back down the steps and placed it at the top of the tree.

CeCe squealed with delight. "Now we just need presents!"

Worry flashed on Kaylie's face, and Mitch grimaced. Obviously, Kaylie hadn't bought gifts for her daughter.

Dammit. Every kid ought to have something under the tree on Christmas morning.

"What do you want Santa to bring you?" Mitch asked CeCe.

"I told you—an orange kitty," CeCe exclaimed in a voice that asked how he could possibly forget. "And a new cowboy hat and pink cowboy boots so I can be a cowboy like you."

Her comment tore at him. He didn't want to care about Kaylie or her daughter, but it was impossible not to let CeCe's childhood excitement affect him.

Kaylie rubbed CeCe's back. "Okay, kiddo, it's been a busy day, but it's time for bed now."

CeCe poked her lips into a pout. "But I wants Mr. Mitch to see the horsie upstairs."

Mitch frowned, but CeCe latched onto his hand and dragged him toward the stairs. Kaylie followed, reminding her daughter that it was bedtime.

Then CeCe pulled him into the room where she was sleeping. His son's room.

Surprise twisted his gut at the sight of the quilt his grandmother had made for him. It now covered Todd's bed.

All of Todd's toy animals and ponies were lined up on the floor as if CeCe had been playing rodeo just like Todd used to do.

He had packed those away for a reason.

"Where did you get those?"

"The boy who lives here showed 'em to me," CeCe said. "They was under the bed."

"What boy?" Mitch asked, his tone tinged with a harshness that he hadn't meant to reveal.

CeCe picked up the horse and made a whinnying sound. "Todd. He said I could play with them."

What the hell was she talking about? Todd was dead and gone . . .

And he hadn't told Kaylie or CeCe about him.

"You shouldn't have gotten them out." Mitch couldn't

breathe. He had to get out of the room.

Away from this woman and child who'd taken over his house and his life. Away from the memories and pain and the little girl who'd spoken his son's name as if she knew him.

———

KAYLIE TWISTED HER HANDS together as Mitch stomped from the room. Why was he angry at CeCe for playing with the toys?

Her daughter burst into tears, then grabbed her rag doll and clutched it to her. "I'm sorry, Mommy. I didn't mean to make Mr. Mitch mad."

Kaylie pulled her daughter into her arms. "Shh, it's all right, sweetie. You didn't do anything wrong."

"I thoughts Mr. Mitch would like the ponies. Todd said he gave them to him."

Kaylie frowned and massaged CeCe's back. "What?"

"Todd, the little boy that used to live here," CeCe said matter-of-factly. "He said Mr. Mitch used to play with him and the ponies."

Kaylie wiped a tear from CeCe's cheek. If that was true, Mitch had lied. He had known the owner. Unless it was a neighbor's child. "Tell me about Todd."

CeCe pointed to the bed. "He used to sleep in my bed. He likes the way I set up the ponies." She gulped. "Horseshoe was *his* horsie."

"When did you see Todd?"

"When we moved in," CeCe said. "He comes to play with me sometimes."

She'd thought Todd was an imaginary friend, but CeCe made him sound real. Was a neighbor's child sneaking into the house somehow? If he was, where did he live? The ranch was acres from anybody else. "Where is he now?"

CeCe bit her lip. "In heaven where Daddy is."

A cold chill washed over Kaylie. What was her daughter saying? That she'd seen a little boy's ghost?

MITCH LEANED OVER THE wooden railing of the pen, pain rocking through him. He struggled for a breath and fought the tears that had hounded him since he'd buried his son but lost the battle.

How had CeCe known about Todd?

Hell . . . he shouldn't have yelled at the kid, but her words had cut him to the bone.

He scrubbed at his eyes, angry that he'd lost control and wishing he'd run Kaylie and CeCe off the moment he'd seen them get out of their damn Pathfinder.

He should tell them to leave tonight. That he never wanted to see them again.

Footsteps sounded behind them, and he jerked his head around, suddenly remembering that a killer might be after Kaylie and CeCe.

But Kaylie walked toward him, arms folded, her mouth set in a grim line.

He turned away, hands clenching the wood railing as he

dug his boot into the dirt. The last thing he wanted was for her to see him fall apart.

Kaylie walked up beside him and leaned against the rail. "What was that all about? You hurt CeCe's feelings."

Anger hardened his insides. These two had no idea what they were doing to him. Making him remember.

Making him feel again.

He wanted the numbness back, the nights of burying his head in a bottle with no little girl or woman looking to him for help.

"I'm sorry, but she had no right to snoop around."

"She wasn't snooping," Kaylie said, her tone defensive like a mother lion protecting her cub. "We found the quilt in the attic, and she found the toys under the bed."

"They were under the bed for a reason."

"What reason?" CeCe asked. "Who is she hurting by playing with them?"

"They don't belong to her," Mitch growled.

"No, but whoever they did belong to left them behind so they obviously didn't care enough to take them."

Anguish squeezed the air from his lungs. "How did you find out about Todd?"

Kaylie cleared her throat. "Tonight is the first I've heard of him. I heard her talking in the bedroom before, but I thought she'd invented an imaginary friend."

"She knew his name."

"Who is he?" Kaylie asked.

Mitch's shoulders shook again as he grappled for words.

Kaylie laid a hand on his back to soothe him. "Talk to me, Mitch. Tell me what's going on."

"Todd was my son," Mitch said through clenched teeth.

Kaylie's breath whispered out. "Your son?"

Mitch angled his face toward her, his heart hammering. "Yes. He died a few months ago. Those were his toys."

Kaylie's eyes softened with compassion, although confusion flickered there as well. "I'm sorry, Mitch. What happened to him?"

He didn't want to divulge the truth and see the disappointment in her eyes. She'd know then that he'd failed his family.

Then again, maybe she needed to know so she'd leave and take her daughter far, far away.

"He and my wife were murdered," Mitch said, his voice cold with anger.

Kaylie pressed a hand to her fist to stifle a gasp. "Oh, my god, Mitch, I'm so sorry." She squeezed his shoulder, but he tensed, and she quickly removed it.

"I don't understand. Why were your son's toys in the ranch house?"

It was time for both of their lies to come out. "Because he lived here, Kaylie."

Her eyes widened in shock at the sound of her real name.

"He lived here?"

He nodded. "This ranch belongs to me."

KAYLIE'S EARS RANG AS Mitch's words reverberated in her head. First, he'd called her by her real name.

Meaning he knew who she was?

And second, he owned the Double M.

The truth hit her, making her feel ill inside. He not only owned the ranch, but he'd lied to her.

Why? Because he was working for Larry Buckham?

"You made me think you were just a hired hand," Kaylie said, instantly backing away. "And how do you know my name?"

"You lied to me, too," he said. "Now it's time we both came clean."

Kaylie shuddered. She'd actually trusted this man when she thought she'd never trust anyone else again.

She eased toward the house. She had to pack her things and get her and CeCe out of here. CeCe.

God.

Her daughter would be devastated. She loved the ranch, the horses. All she'd wanted was a real Christmas.

And now she had to ruin it.

Mitch caught her arm just as she reached the porch. "Going to run again, Kaylie?"

She trembled. "You don't understand. I have to protect my daughter. And if you're working for Buckham—"

"I'm not," Mitch said sharply. "For God's sake, I'm a Texas Ranger."

Shock waves rolled through her. "What?"

He gripped her harder when she tried to pull away. "I'm a Texas Ranger. My family was killed because of my job. That's why I'm selling the ranch."

Kaylie's chest constricted. "Why didn't you tell me that when I first came here?" Humiliation heated her face. "And why did you stand by and let me fix up the house?"

"I let you stay because you looked scared," he said, his voice cracking. "And because you lied to me. That made me curious. I wanted the truth."

Betrayal knifed through her. "So, you investigated me?"

"You were on my property under false pretenses. I had to know what I was dealing with."

She felt like a fool. "Now you do," she said, jerking away from him. "But don't worry. You don't have to *deal* with us. We'll leave first thing in the morning. And I'll put everything in the house back the way I found it."

"You don't have to do that. You were right. The house will show better now."

"Fine. I'll go pack then."

"Where are you going to run now, Kaylie?"

Tears burned the back of her eyelids. "I don't know, but my daughter and I aren't your problem."

"The hell you're not," he snapped. "If someone's after you, I can't let you go off on your own. It's too dangerous."

"You can't stop me." She rushed up the porch steps and reached for the doorknob. She had to stand on her own two feet, take her daughter someplace far away from here and Bend Creek where another family had just been murdered.

"What about CeCe?" he asked in a gruff voice. "What about Santa Claus and Christmas and the kitten she wanted?"

Kaylie felt as if she'd been punched in the chest. She gripped the door handle and bowed her head, her lungs straining for air as she struggled to control her frustration.

Mitch's footsteps echoed behind her. "I know you're angry with me, but don't take CeCe away. She deserves to have Santa surprise her with presents. Especially this year when she just lost her father."

Kaylie wanted to ask him what he knew about her daughter or children in general. But she'd seen the tears in his eyes when he'd confessed that he'd lost a son.

No wonder he'd been so upset when he'd seen CeCe playing with his little boy's toys. This must be the first Christmas Mitch would have without him.

She couldn't imagine living without CeCe.

———•———

DAMMIT, HE SHOULD LET them go.

But he'd failed to keep his own family safe, and now this woman and child were in danger, and he couldn't stand to think of them on their own facing a killer.

"That's not fair," Kaylie said in a haunted whisper. "The only reason I stayed here was to give CeCe Christmas."

Mitch gently turned Kaylie to look at him. "Then don't go. We'll give her Christmas, and I'll protect you both until your husband's killer is caught."

Even as he made the promise though, doubts dogged him. He'd promised to take care of Sally and Todd and failed them.

What if he failed Kaylie and her daughter?

CHAPTER 11

KAYLIE WANTED TO TRUST Mitch. God knows she needed help and everyone else had let her down.

Or they'd died trying to protect her.

She didn't want any harm to come to Mitch. He'd obviously suffered a terrible tragedy in his own life.

"Mitch, I appreciate the offer, but the last two men who guarded me and CeCe ended up dead."

Mitch's expression hardened. "Don't worry about me."

The deep sorrow in his voice moved her more than anything else.

Mitch led her to the porch swing, and they settled inside it. "I won't let you go out there alone, Kaylie. Tell me exactly what happened."

Kaylie gripped his hand like a lifeline and relayed the details of the night her husband was murdered.

"You identified Larry Buckham even though you didn't actually see his face?"

She nodded. "I recognized his voice. And those eyes. I'd never forget the cold way he looked at me and CeCe."

"The police believed he was the serial murderer killing families around Austin? Other than your testimony, did they have evidence at the trial to support that theory?"

"The MO was the same," Kaylie said. "And he had no alibi for the night of the other murders. He also used the same kind of weapon."

"All circumstantial."

"Yes, but the photos of Joe's body and the bedroom where he was murdered were pretty convincing."

"Then why is Buckham's attorney making suggestions that you killed your husband?"

Kaylie's breath caught. "You really did investigate me, didn't you?"

"Yes, but not to hurt you, Kaylie."

"You think I killed my husband?"

"If I believed you were guilty, I would have turned you in."

His faith in her triggered another well of emotions. It had been so long since she'd leaned on anyone that she didn't know how to respond.

"Were you and Joe having problems in your marriage?" Mitch asked quietly.

Kaylie shook her head. "No. Although thinking back, he was distant the last few months and took several out of town trips. But I just thought he was preoccupied with work."

"Any financial problems?"

She released a weary sigh as if she didn't want to discuss the past.

"Kaylie, I can't help you if I don't know the truth."

"I didn't think so, but when I looked back at some paperwork I found after he died, I discovered an account I didn't know about."

Mitch pushed the swing back and forth with his feet, tension stretching between them. "Is there any chance he was killed over the money in that account?"

"I honestly don't know."

"What happened after the trial?"

Kaylie remembered the grief-stricken months. "CeCe and I tried to put our life back together. But then Buckham escaped in that prison break, and we went into protective custody."

"Then what happened?"

"One night we were at the safe house and someone threw a pipe bomb inside. Arnold, the man guarding us, rushed us toward the back door, but it was a setup and he was shot."

"You and CeCe escaped?"

Kaylie trembled as she remembered how terrified she and CeCe had been. "CeCe was crying and screaming, but we ran to the car, and I just drove," Kaylie said. "I had to get us away. Later when I stopped to call Rafferty, the marshal in charge of our protective detail, I heard a shot fired on the other end of the line. He . . . was shot, too."

Kaylie didn't realize tears were streaming down her cheeks until Mitch pulled her into his arms. Exhausted, she collapsed against him.

Tomorrow she would be strong. But tonight, she gave in and let him hold her.

———••———

Mitch cradled Kaylie to him, soothing her with gentle touches and whispered words as he imagined the terror CeCe had felt.

She had not only witnessed her father's murder, but also another man's. And she knew that a bad man was after her mother and her.

Kaylie sighed against him, such a weary sound that his lungs strained for air. More than anything he wanted to make her feel secure.

He tilted her head up and looked into her eyes. "It's going to be okay, Kaylie. I promise."

Hope and desire flickered in her expression, then she parted her lips. Tension stretched between them for a heartbeat before she touched his jaw, then leaned up and kissed him.

Mitch had been consumed with pain and an emptiness that had broken him. But Kaylie's trust and her sweet lips against his brought him back to life.

He wanted more.

Yet he had to be careful. He couldn't take advantage of her.

She drew his face closer, and deepened the kiss, inviting his tongue to play with hers.

Hunger heated his blood, and he threaded his fingers into her hair, desperate to be closer to her. He rubbed her back, then trailed kisses down her ear and her neck, inhaling her feminine scent.

But reality interceded, and he remembered that a madman might be watching, so he slowly ended the kiss.

"You should go inside," he said gruffly.

Kaylie's gaze met his, the need in her eyes twisting him inside out. "Come with me, Mitch."

"Kaylie—"

"Please. I don't want to be alone tonight."

Neither did he.

But he couldn't forget they were in danger. He hurried to his truck, retrieved his shotgun, then followed her inside and locked the door.

Ignoring the warning voice in his head, he stopped at the master bedroom door while she checked on CeCe. When she emerged from the room, he expected her to change her mind.

It would be the smart thing to do.

But she gathered his hand in hers and pulled him into the bedroom. Mitch closed the door when they entered, determined to give Kaylie the opportunity to stop if she wanted.

"Mitch?"

"I'm trying to do the right thing," he said in a low voice.

"You are. You're taking care of me and CeCe tonight. That's all I expect, all I need."

He wanted it, too. Although he had a sinking feeling that tonight might not be enough. That if she planned to run tomorrow, he'd stop her.

Silencing the doubts in his mind, he gave into the need and desire her words evoked and kissed her again.

One touch of his lips on hers led to heated touches, and he slowly stripped her blouse and trailed kisses along her throat and neck. She threaded her fingers into his hair and rubbed her foot against his calf.

Desire bolted through him. His body hardened to an aching need, and he cupped her breast in his hand. She whispered his name, the soft sound tender with longing.

Knowing she wanted him with the intensity he felt for her drove him to strip her bra and gingerly tease her nipples with his thumb. She moaned his name, and he lowered his mouth, tugged one plump nipple into his mouth and suckled her.

She raked her hands down his back, clinging to him as her body shivered against him. His sex throbbed, hardening and bulging against the fly of his jeans, but he wanted to give her pleasure more than he wanted to take it for himself.

He backed her toward the bed and lowered her onto the mattress, kissing her again as he tugged at her jeans. She pulled at his shirt, unbuttoning it frantically and shoving it over his shoulders.

Heat blazed between them, clothes flying to the floor as they caressed and loved each other. Naked body against naked body, the friction was almost more than Mitch could bear.

She reached down to cup his sex, but he pushed her hand away, laving her breasts again, then he dropped kisses down her belly to her inner thighs. Exhilarated when she whimpered his name, he parted her thighs and drove his tongue between her legs.

Her sweet feminine taste intensified his hunger, and he

flicked his tongue along her clit, teasing her unmercifully until her body began to quiver with sensations.

"Mitch . . ."

He loved the way she said his name as if she wanted him inside her.

He wanted to be there, too, to fill her and make her his.

The thought startled him, and he started to pull away. But her hands clawed at him as her body convulsed with her release. He savored the taste of her, rising on his knees as he dug a condom from his pocket, rolled it on, then guided his cock toward her center.

She lifted her hips, begging for him, and he obeyed, sliding his thick length inside her, pulling out and thrusting again. He gripped her bottom and angled her so he could reach deeper, his body gliding against hers, building a rhythm as they caressed and loved one another.

Kaylie clung to Mitch, her body quivering with erotic sensations that drove her over the edge into bliss. She whispered his name in a throaty moan, gripping his hips as he pounded inside her.

Mitch was a big man, strong and powerful, fierce in his loving, but tender in the way he held her and looked into her eyes as his release claimed him.

Before he could pull out, she knew she wanted him again. That in spite of her fear and the situation, she was falling for him.

But he had lied to her and investigated her. Had stood by while she cleaned and decorated his house and said nothing.

Doubts and anger warred in her mind, but he kissed her again, and she forgot everything but the feel of his hands touching her and his weight on top of her.

When he finally rolled off of her and cradled her in his arms, she closed her eyes and fell into a contented sleep.

And for the first time in months, she dreamt of a future for her and CeCe that didn't include murder.

THE TEXAS RANGER WAS screwing the bitch.

Buckham adjusted his binoculars, furious.

Shit. How was he going to kill her with that Ranger all over her?

The newsfeed buzzed in his earphone, the reporter citing that another family murder had occurred the night before. Over in Bend Creek.

Just a few miles away.

The damn Family Man had laid low while *he* was in jail. He'd probably laughed his ass off knowing that he'd gotten away with three murders while another man took the blame.

Buckham grunted, lit a cigarette and took a puff. For Whittaker's murder, he'd have done time. But he wouldn't have been sitting on death row if not for the other murders.

Murders he had nothing to do with.

The dumbass cops had to be set straight. First, he'd kill

Whittaker's wife. Then he might just have to find the real Family Man killer himself and point him out to the stupid fucking cops.

CHAPTER 12

ITCH STARED AT THE ceiling, his pulse clamoring at the
sound of Kaylie's soft breathing.

He shouldn't have made love to her.

But how he could not have?

The hunger in her eyes had mirrored the need and desire
consuming him.

But guilt nagged at him, and he felt as if he'd betrayed his
dead wife and son by having Kaylie and CeCe into their home.

CeCe's comment about his son taunted him. She'd said that
Todd told her she could play with the toys.

Where had she come up with that?

Confused by his warring emotions, he slowly extracted himself from Kaylie, slid from bed and walked to the bathroom.
After he disposed of the condom, he yanked on his clothes and
eased from the room.

Crawling back in bed with Kaylie teased at his mind, but he couldn't. When Buckham was back in jail, she would leave and move on with her life.

And he would be here.

Alone with his grief and memories of Todd. And now memories of watching Kaylie and her daughter decorate his house and the Christmas tree, the two of them filling the house with laughter and the smell of fried chicken and cookies baking.

It was almost more than he could bear.

She couldn't leave yet anyway. Buckham was still on the loose, probably hunting for another victim. The idea of a cold-blooded killer getting his hands on her or her daughter resurrected his instincts as a Texas Ranger.

He couldn't let down his guard. Kaylie had been here several days now. For all he knew Buckham might have already tracked her to the ranch.

KAYLIE ROLLED OVER IN bed, erotic memories of the night before suffusing her. Last night in Mitch's arms gave her hope that everything would be all right again.

But the bed beside her was empty.

Did Mitch have regrets?

It's for the best, she told herself. She wouldn't want CeCe to find them together.

She slipped from bed, showered and dressed, the calendar mocking her. Two days until Christmas.

CeCe had added a cowboy hat and pink cowboy boots to her Christmas list. She had to figure out a way to buy them.

CeCe was still sleeping, so she sewed a new outfit for CeCe's doll, made a blanket from scraps, and a pillow, and then fashioned a baby carrier for the doll.

By the time she finished, CeCe tiptoed down the steps in her pajamas. Kaylie cooked biscuits and sausage for breakfast, and CeCe wolfed hers down. Mitch had disappeared, probably to check on something on the ranch.

A few minutes later, he appeared in the kitchen, looking freshly shaven and sexy in his western shirt and jeans.

God, he was more man than any man should be.

CeCe raced over to him and grabbed his big hand. Hers looked impossibly small next to his rugged palm. "Can I ride Horseshoe again today?"

"Maybe later. I thought we might ride into town this morning and do a little Christmas shopping."

CeCe motioned for Mitch to squat down, then whispered something in his ear. When he pulled back, he grinned at her.

"That's a great idea, sweatpea."

"What are you two whispering about?" Kaylie asked.

CeCe bounced from foot to foot, looking sheepish.

"Nothing," Mitch said with a wink toward her daughter. "You can't be nosing around too much at Christmas."

Kaylie blushed at his teasing tone. CeCe must have asked him to help her shop. The fact that Mitch would do something so sweet for her daughter melted her heart.

Mitch grabbed a biscuit and sausage from the counter. "Go

get dressed, CeCe. We'll leave in a few minutes."

"Yippee!" CeCe skipped toward the steps, and Kaylie wanted to hug Mitch.

"Thank you for being so kind to her," Kaylie said. *And to me.*

"She's a great kid. She deserves that much."

"Yes, she does," Kaylie said. "And I need to buy the gifts on her Christmas wish list. But we have to be careful in town so no one recognizes us."

"They'll be looking for you and CeCe alone, not the three of us."

"True." Kaylie wiped down the counter. "But I'm still nervous."

Mitch cleared his throat. "Trust me. I won't let anything happen to either of you."

Kaylie nodded, desperate to touch him again. She did trust Mitch.

But she didn't trust herself. Because she was falling in love with Mitch.

A man who was still mourning the loss of his wife and son.

And she couldn't even fantasize about a future when her life was such a mess.

When keeping her daughter safe was the only thing that really mattered.

MITCH STAYED ALERT AS he drove Kaylie and CeCe into town. CeCe wore a ball cap, and Kaylie tied a scarf around her hair, but she seemed nervous and twitchy as they entered the department store.

"CeCe and I have a little errand to run." He gave Kaylie a throwaway cell he'd bought at the gas station on the way in, obviously offering her time to shop for CeCe's gifts. "Call me if you see anything suspicious."

"I will." She caught Mitch's arm. "Thanks, Mitch."

He pointed to an elderly woman with graying hair, then whispered, "Let Vera help you. She'll know where the pink boots are."

He took CeCe's hand, and they left Kaylie with Vera. CeCe chattered on and on about how pretty the decorations in the store looked as they found the jewelry section.

"I wants to get Mommy a Christmas pin," CeCe said. "One that sparkles."

"She'll love that," Mitch said.

A teenager with striped red hair grinned at CeCe when she described what she wanted. "I know just where to find it."

The teen showed CeCe a display, and CeCe's eyes lit up. There were candy canes, Christmas trees, wreaths, and angels that glittered.

"The angel," CeCe said. "Cause Mommy said Daddy is an angel watching over us."

The reminder of her father made Mitch look around for Buckham. CeCe counted out the money she'd saved from helping her mother do chores, and the salesclerk boxed up the pin and handed it to CeCe.

Mitch's cell phone buzzed, and he checked the number. Micah Hardin. He'd call him back. "Hey, sweet pea, let's find your mother."

"'kay," CeCe said in a low voice as she tugged at his hand. "But don't tell her 'bout the pin. It's a surprise."

Mitch made a gesture with his fingers as if he was locking the secret in a vault.

They found Kaylie with a shopping bag and a smile on her face.

She looked so damn beautiful that Mitch wanted to wrap her in his arms and never let her go.

"Done?" he asked.

She nodded. "How about you two?"

"Yep."

CeCe's eyes sparkled with joy at her secret.

"Let's go to the diner for lunch."

Kaylie bit her lip and looked around, anxious again. But he looped his arm around her shoulder and took CeCe's hand and led the way. When they entered the diner, he ushered them to the back booth so they wouldn't be visible to anyone who entered.

"I need to make a phone call. I'll be right back." He hurried outside to phone Micah. "What's going on, Hardin?"

"The sheriff over in Bend Creek arrested a man he believes is the Family Man killer."

Mitch inhaled sharply. "Is it Larry Buckham?"

"No," Micah said. "But I thought you might be interested."

He was. "Thanks. I'll ride over and see what kind of evidence the sheriff has."

If Buckham hadn't killed the families, it might mean Kaylie was wrong about Buckham, that he hadn't killed her husband.

Or that there were two different killers. If that was true and she was right about Buckham, Kaylie and CeCe were still in danger.

———————

KAYLIE SENSED MITCH'S TENSION as he paid the bill, and they walked out to his vehicle.

"What's wrong?"

He gestured toward CeCe in the back seat. "We'll talk when we get home."

Realizing he wanted to protect her daughter, she simply nodded. But her stomach churned the entire way back to the ranch.

He'd used the word home—but as much as she wanted it to be, the ranch wasn't her home. It belonged to Mitch. Would he sell it when they left?

When they arrived back at the ranch, CeCe insisted on wrapping the gift she'd bought, so Kaylie left her in the kitchen with tape and wrapping paper while she walked Mitch outside.

"I'm going to Bend Creek to talk to the sheriff," Mitch said. "They arrested a man they believe killed those other families near Austin."

Kaylie folded her arms. She didn't know what to think. "It wasn't Larry Buckham?"

"No. That's why I want to question him myself."

Doubts assailed Kaylie. Could she have been wrong about Buckham?

"I haven't seen anyone around here." Mitch retrieved his rifle from his truck. "But I want you to take this just in case."

"That's okay, Mitch. I have a pistol upstairs."

"You know how to shoot?"

She nodded.

"Then keep it with you until I return."

Kaylie agreed, but her nerves were on edge as Mitch drove away. She ran up the stairs, retrieved her gun and tucked it on the top shelf in the pantry so CeCe couldn't reach it, but so she could grab it if needed.

She paced the den, contemplating her situation.

She had to find a way to prove that she hadn't killed her husband. If she did, could she and Mitch make a life together?

Or was he still in love with his dead wife?

———

MITCH SHOOK HANDS WITH Sheriff Aiden Turner at the Bend Creek sheriff's office. "You think you have the Family Man murderer in custody?"

Sheriff Turner, a tall, lean-looking cowboy with sandy hair, nodded. "His prints match prints found on the bullet we pulled from the wall at the family's house."

A common mistake. The perp had probably worn gloves when he'd shot the families but hadn't when he'd loaded his weapon.

"Did he confess?"

"Not yet. We just picked him up this morning. His name is Frank Fittinger."

"I'd like to be included in the interrogation."

Sheriff Turner raised a brow. "What's your interest here?"

"I've been following the manhunt for Larry Buckham. He was convicted of murdering Joe Whittaker and trying to kill his wife and child."

"Yes, I know. The DA implied that he was also the serial killer murdering families. If we nail the man in my cell, that'll blow that case to hell."

"Exactly."

Mitch followed Turner to the back where he retrieved the prisoner, a stout, balding guy with pocked skin and a missing front tooth. He smelled like cigarettes, stale beer and sweat and looked like a man who'd seen trouble before.

Fittinger muttered an obscenity as Turner opened the cell door and hauled him toward the interrogation room.

"You ain't got no right to lock me up," Fittinger bellowed.

"I've got every right," Sheriff Turner said firmly.

The sheriff shoved the man into a chair, then leaned against the table, arms folded. Mitch settled across from the beefy guy, scrutinizing his features. Ruddy skin. Dirt beneath his fingernails. Tattered shirt. A tattoo of the word mother on his upper arm.

Sheriff Fittinger slapped a file on the desk, then opened it. "You might as well confess, Fittinger. We have your prints on the bullet that killed Horace Lassiter and on the bullets that killed his wife and son."

"You obviously remembered to wear gloves to the crime scene, but when you loaded the ammunition."

Fittinger's bravado crumpled. "Shit."

"Why did you do it?" Sheriff Turner asked.

Fittinger drummed his hands on the scarred table.

Turner laid photos of each of the families in front of the perp. A couple with the last name Sorenson and a teenage boy. Another couple, the Haneys, another teenage son. The Murdocks, one son age thirteen. Then the Whittakers, Kaylie's husband Joe, Kaylie and CeCe.

The couple from Bend Creek, the Lassiters with two teenage boys.

Mitch mentally analyzed the facts they had so far. All the couples had teenage boys, no girls, especially five-year-olds.

The Whittakers didn't fit the pattern of the victimology.

"Those people had everything," Fittinger bellowed. "A family, sons, but they were throwing it all away."

"What do you mean, throwing it all away?" Sheriff Turner asked.

Fittinger yanked at his hair with his fists. "They were getting a divorce," Fittinger shouted. "Throwing the kids to the wolves because they were cheaters and liars."

"Is that what happened to you?" Mitch asked.

Fittinger's face reddened. "My mama loved my daddy, but he cheated and beat me and threw us away."

"So you think the families are better off dead than divorced?"

"They tore their families up, not me." He beat at his chest with his fist, ranting incoherently.

Had Kaylie's husband cheated on her? Had they discussed divorce?

"I didn't kill that Whittaker man," Fittinger snarled. "And

that son of a bitch Larry Buckham had no right taking credit for my murders either."

Mitch considered the victimology. As much as he wanted to believe Fittinger was lying about shooting Joe Whittaker, he believed the man.

Which meant that Kaylie was right, that Larry Buckham had killed her husband. And now he'd escaped prison, he was coming after her.

He told the sheriff he'd talk to him later, then hurried to the front office to call Kaylie.

The phone rang and rang, but she didn't answer.

He hung up, then called again, but the voicemail kicked in.

Heart pounding with fear, he jogged outside to his truck and roared from the parking lot.

⸺ ⸱ ⸺

Kaylie had given CeCe plenty of time to wrap her present. She wished she'd had the time and money to buy Mitch a gift to thank him for all he'd done for them, for allowing them to share his home, but she hadn't.

The cookies she and CeCe baked would have to do.

Knowing the ranch belonged to him made her hope that he would keep it when they were gone. But she had only pleasant memories here, where he had painful memories of the son and wife he'd lost.

"CeCe, are you finished?" Kaylie peeked into the kitchen, frowning when she realized CeCe wasn't at the table.

The back door stood ajar.

Had her daughter slipped out to the barn to see Horseshoe? She wasn't supposed to without an adult, but CeCe loved the horse.

Still, worry seized her. What if she was wrong? What if Buckham had found them?

Suddenly panicked, she raced through the kitchen shouting CeCe's name. But her chest constricted when the man she'd feared stepped from the shadows of the doorway leading to the back stoop.

Sheer terror filled Kaylie as the man clamped his hand over CeCe's mouth and pressed a gun to her head.

CHAPTER 13

CeCe didn't want to die.

She knew she'd go to Heaven and get to see her daddy again. And she had a friend there now, Todd. Well, at least he was on his way there, but he said he couldn't go yet, not till his daddy knew he loved him and wasn't so sad.

If she did have to go now, Todd would show her the ropes, where to play and how to make other kid friends.

But then her mommy would be alone. Unless the bad man killed her, too.

Then they wouldn't get to have Christmas this year.

And she'd never see Horseshoe again or get her kitty cat.

She wondered if God let kids have kitties in heaven.

"Please don't hurt my daughter," Kaylie said. "I'll do whatever you ask, just let her go."

Larry Buckham's jowl twitched with rage. "You made everyone think I killed all those families, but I didn't."

Kaylie strained for a breath. "Then prove it. Hurting me and CeCe is only going to make you look guilty."

CeCe suddenly bit his hand, and the man bellowed and shoved her away from him. Kaylie caught her daughter and pushed her behind her to protect her.

"You little twit!" Buckham shouted as he shook his hand in pain.

"She's just a scared little girl," Kaylie said sharply. "And you're being a bully to her."

He stepped forward with a menacing glare, and Kaylie backed up, one hand on her daughter. If she got the chance, she'd tell CeCe to run.

"You sent me to jail, but your husband got what he deserved."

Kaylie's heart pounded. "No one deserves to be gunned down in front of his child."

"He was stupid and greedy," Buckham snarled. "He tried to blackmail his client for money."

Oh, God . . . Joe. Was that where the money in that separate account had come from?

"That client was you?" Kaylie asked in a shaky voice.

"No, my boss. Your husband learned his secrets and threatened to turn him over to the police. Then he started in with the blackmail."

"So your boss paid you to get rid of his problem," Kaylie said, the truth dawning.

"Exactly." He waved his gun at her.

"Then he hung you out to dry, didn't he?" Kaylie asked. "He let you go to jail and take the fall."

"If it wasn't for you, I never would have been caught," Buckham said. "But I'm not sitting on death row for those other murders."

Behind her, CeCe whimpered, her fingernails digging into Kaylie's arm. "What do you want?"

"The key to his safety deposit box," Buckham said.

"What's in it?" Kaylie asked.

Buckham laughed. "Money, you idiot. With that cash, I can escape the country."

Betrayal shot through Kaylie. On top of the bank account, she hadn't known about, Joe had a safety deposit box that he'd kept from her.

"Give me the key."

"I . . . don't know where it is," Kaylie said. "Joe didn't tell me anything about it."

Buckham jammed the gun toward her face, the barrel staring her in the eyes. "I don't believe you."

Terror stole through Kaylie. "I told you I didn't know about it," Kaylie whispered. "If I did, I'd give you the key."

CeCe tugged at her hand. "Mommy?"

"Shh, baby," Kaylie said softly. "It'll be all right."

"I don't think so," Buckham said. "If you want the kid to live, I need the money."Panic immobilized Kaylie. How much money was in that account? Could she gain access to that foreign account of Joe's?

"Mommy," CeCe said in a small voice. "I gots the key."

Kaylie gasped and looked down at her daughter. "What?"

CeCe's face paled with fear. "I gots the key."

Buckham's evil grin revealed crooked yellow teeth. "Then give it to me, kid, and I'll let you and your mommy go."

Kaylie didn't believe him, but they didn't have a choice. "Where is it, CeCe?"

CeCe pointed to her rag doll lying on the kitchen table. "Daddy put it on a string and made a necklace for my doll. He tolded me to keep it for him."

Kaylie's legs nearly buckled at the very idea of her husband entrusting her daughter with something so dangerous. Why in the world hadn't he told *her* what was going on?

Buckham nudged them both toward the table. "Get it for me, kid."

CeCe released her mother's hand, grabbed the rag doll and held it out to Buckham. Buckham fiddled with the doll, then yanked the string from around its neck. CeCe had tucked the key inside the doll's dress, but it glinted in the light as he held it up to examine it.

"Thanks, kid."

Kaylie squared her shoulders. "You got what you came for, now leave us alone."

Buckham's jowls jiggled as he shook his head." Sorry, lady, but I can't do that."

He gestured toward the door. "Now, walk."

Kaylie clutched her daughter to her and did as he said, mentally searching for a way to escape. He forced them to walk to his black sedan, then opened the trunk and shoved them inside.

Kaylie pulled her daughter into her arms as he slammed the trunk closed.

God help them. How could she save them now?

MITCH RACED ONTO THE ranch, his heart hammering with fear.

He'd called Kaylie a dozen times on the way back, and she hadn't answered. Something was wrong.

The Pathfinder still sat where she'd left it earlier. He threw the truck into park and ran inside the farmhouse, yelling for them. "Kaylie? CeCe?"

An eerie quiet fell over the house, the furnace rumbling and creaking as it worked to warm the chill from the rooms. He rushed through the den, then the kitchen, praying he'd find them. CeCe's present sat on the table, wrapped and covered with scotch tape, but there was no one in the room.

He ran into the hall and up the steps, checking each of the rooms, but they were empty as well.

Maybe they were in the barn petting Horseshoe. They might have even saddled up and taken a ride.

He hurried out the door and ran to the barn, calling their names again. When he stepped inside, the horses whinnied, and Horseshoe rapped at the door to her stall.

"Where are they, buddy?" Images of Kaylie and CeCe hurt or bleeding taunted him.

Then images of his wife and son, dead, flashed behind his eyes.

No . . . he couldn't have found Kaylie and CeCe only to lose them now.

He raced back to the kitchen, hoping Kaylie had left a note, that she and CeCe had simply gone for a walk.

But when he looked in the kitchen again, he spotted scuff marks on the floor as if someone had dragged their shoes. He followed the marks to the back porch and noticed a boot print.

A large print, the size of a man's shoe.

Cold dread filled him.

Buckham must have found them and taken them somewhere.

He punched Micah's number and relayed what had happened, filling him in on his conversation with Fittinger.

"Alert authorities to look for Buckham," he said. "Kaylie and CeCe are in terrible danger."

Mitch ended the call, his adrenaline pumping. He drove his truck out to the helipad he'd built on the south end of the property for his personal helicopter, climbed in and geared up. Seconds later, he lifted off, his gaze sweeping his property and the road for anything suspicious.

Dammit, he wished to hell he knew what kind of car Buckham was driving.

The chopper rose above the treetops, yet he stayed low enough to scan the area, aware daylight had waned. Night was falling and would soon make visibility more difficult.

Even though it was winter, his land looked rich, his pastures waiting for livestock. His grandfather had loved this land, had claimed the rich earth and soil were part of him.

How could he sell it to a stranger?

He'd thought he couldn't live here without his son, but Kaylie and CeCe had filled the farmhouse with laughter and the warmth of a real family.

Suddenly he spotted a black sedan weaving onto a side road that led to the river. The old campground that used to be there was overgrown, the buildings rotting.

Another car, a shiny Mercedes, was parked near the river.

Mitch guided the chopper to the right, following it, his anxiety rising as the sedan pulled to a stop. A big man he recognized from photos as Larry Buckham climbed from the front, then strode over to the Mercedes.

The windows in the Mercedes were tinted so dark, Mitch couldn't see who he was talking to, but Buckham leaned close to the window in conversation, then returned to the sedan.

A minute later, he opened the car door, gripped the door edge and steering wheel, and he pushed the car toward the river.

Mitch lost his breath. Obviously, Buckham was going to ditch the car so no one could find it.

But where were Kaylie and CeCe?

The truth hit him with the force of a bullet. They were locked in the trunk.

Buckham was going to leave them there to drown while he escaped with the man waiting in the Mercedes.

Kaylie hugged CeCe to her, fear nearly paralyzing her. She had to save her daughter.

But how?

She had no idea where they were. They'd driven away from the ranch and turned onto a road that was rough with potholes.

Maybe a dirt road?

They'd passed the river—she'd heard water running. And now . . .

Now the car had stopped. Buckham had gotten out for a minute, but the car was moving again, only slowly this time.

The sound of water gushing around them made her breath catch. Dear God . . . the car felt as if it was sinking. Water gurgled, but the engine wasn't running.

"Mommy!" CeCe cried.

Kaylie fought panic as she realized the car was sinking into the water.

And they were trapped.

Survival instincts battled with cold terror. There had to be a way out.

Didn't cars have a latch in the trunk so you could open the trunk from the inside?

"CeCe, honey, Mommy needs to see if I can find a way to open the trunk."

CeCe sniffled but nodded against her. Kaylie kissed her daughter's hair, then released her and frantically ran her hands over the floor, the sides, then the top of the inside of the trunk.

There had to be a latch . . . if there wasn't, she and CeCe were going to drown and no one would ever find them.

CHAPTER 14

Mitch spotted a clearing a half mile from the spot where Buckham was pushing the car into the river and landed the chopper. He called Micah to alert him that he'd spotted Buckham and to send backup.

Terrified Kaylie and CeCe were in that trunk, he grabbed his rifle for backup, his other hand securing his Sig Sauer as he jumped from the helicopter. He ran through the brush, closing the distance between him and the sedan, determined to catch Buckham.

He slowed as he neared the Mercedes, his breath puffing out as he snuck up on the vehicle. Buckham was just climbing in the passenger side when Mitch stepped from the foliage.

He raised the rifle. "It's over, Buckham. You're under arrest."

Buckham froze at the door, then leveled him with a challenging look. "I'm not going back to prison."

"Then you'll go to your grave," Mitch said. "If Kaylie and her little girl are in that car, that'd be my choice anyway."

Buckham lifted a hand as if he was going to surrender, but a gun glinted in the dim light, and Mitch fired. The bullet hit Buckham between the eyes, and he dropped like a sack of flour.

The driver of the Mercedes gunned the engine, but Mitch fired at the driver's side. The bullet pinged off the car door, and the driver sped up, but Mitch rushed forward and fired again. This time the bullet shattered the driver's window.

Mitch fired another shot at the driver. The Mercedes plunged into a tree with a loud crash. Mitch kept his gun aimed as he slowly approached the vehicle. When he was close enough to open the driver's door, he aimed the gun inside the window. A heavyset man was slumped at the wheel, blood oozing from his neck where Mitch had shot him.

Mitch used two fingers to check the man's pulse.

He was dead.

Mitch would find out who the man was later. Right now he had to save Kaylie and CeCe.

Deja vu of being shot and careening into the river where his wife and son died hit him. It was happening again.

Jesus. He couldn't let Kaylie and CeCe drown.

But the sedan was almost immersed in the water. He dropped his rifle and Sig by the edge of the river, kicked off his boots, tossed his hat to the ground, then plunged into the water.

He dove beneath the surface, swam to the car and searched for the lever to open the trunk. The water ebbed around him, slowly seeping into the car. He jerked and yanked at the trunk, but it wouldn't budge.

Adrenaline surged through him, and he swam to the driver's side. The door was ajar, so he jerked at it until he opened enough to reach inside.

He fumbled around the dash in search of an automatic trunk opener and found one on the left-hand side of the seat. He pushed at it until it lifted, then he swam to the back of the sedan again.

His lungs were straining for air, his muscles pushed to the limit as he pried the top of the trunk open.

Kaylie's eyes widened in relief, then panic as water rushed inside. He grabbed her and CeCe and pulled them from the inside.

Kaylie pushed CeCe into his arms, and he nodded in understanding, then cradled her to him and swam to the surface. Kaylie was right behind him, and they both plunged above water, gasping for air at the same time.

CeCe gasped, sputtering water and coughing as he hauled her to the embankment and climbed out. He lay her gently on the ground, then ran back and helped Kaylie.

She staggered, water dripping from her clothes and hair, then collapsed onto the ground beside CeCe.

"Mommy!" CeCe cried.

"I'm here, baby." Kaylie dragged her daughter into her arms and soothed her.

Mitch called for an ambulance, then cradled both of them next to him, trying to warm them by rubbing their arms and hands, while they waited for the medics.

KAYLIE SHIVERED, GRATEFUL THAT she and CeCe were alive as she burrowed against Mitch.

"It's over," he whispered. "Buckham is dead, and so is the man who helped him."

"It was Joe's fault," Kaylie said, anger mounting inside her. "He got greedy and blackmailed one of his clients. That's the reason Buckham shot him."

"He confessed?"

She nodded. "Apparently Joe hid money in a safety deposit box, and Buckham and the man he worked for wanted it back."

CeCe gulped on a sob. "I'm sorry, Mommy. Daddy told me not to tell."

Kaylie hugged her. "He told you not to tell me what?"

"About the money," CeCe said tearfully. "I saw him put it in his gym bag, but he said it was our secret."

How dare Joe use her daughter like that.

She wished with all her might that he was alive so she could vent her rage at him.

"It's not your fault," Mitch said softly to CeCe. "Sweetpea, the bad man can't hurt you or your mommy ever again."

Then they could go home, Kaylie realized, as the ambulance siren wailed and screeched to a stop in the clearing near the cars.

Except the thought of leaving Mitch made her chest constrict.

"Thank you, Mitch," she said softly.

He nodded, but his face looked grim. Was he thinking the

same thing she was—that now Buckham was caught it was time for her and CeCe to leave the ranch so he could sell it and move on with his life?

THE NEXT FEW HOURS were exhausting. Kaylie didn't want to go to the hospital, but Mitch insisted she and CeCe be examined by the doctor. The threat of hypothermia along with almost drowning didn't sit well in his gut.

Micah handled notifying the medical examiner and local sheriff, and while the ambulance transported Kaylie and CeCe to the hospital for a check-up, he tried to tie up the details of the case.

They identified the dead man in the Mercedes as Lester Hubanks, a well-known financial entrepreneur who was being investigated for money laundering. Mitch's fellow Ranger, Sgt. Alex Townsend found the money Buckham had wanted in the safety deposit box Joe Whittaker had arranged.

Mitch explained to the authorities and Buckham's attorney about Fittinger's confession. Sheriff Turner had the Family Man killer in custody. Apparently, Buckham had used the serial killer's MO to throw off the police when he murdered Whittaker.

Coupled with the fact that Buckham had held Kaylie and her daughter at gunpoint and tried to kill them, Kaylie was cleared of suspicion.

Buckham's attorney was also charged with aiding and abetting a felon in his prison escape.

Kaylie's only mistake was trusting the man she'd married.

Just as Sally had trusted him.

He'd let her and Todd down. But at least he'd saved Kaylie and CeCe.

Not that they could take his family's place.

Todd would always live in his memories and his heart.

THE NEXT NIGHT CeCe could barely sleep she was so excited. All day her mommy and Mr. Mitch had hugged her and assured her the bad men were gone forever.

They read Christmas stories and sung holiday tunes, and Mr. Mitch even drove them to a little church in town where they listened to the preacher man talk about Jesus being born in a manger.

CeCe asked her mommy if she was born in a manger, but her mommy said no, that she was born in a hospital.

CeCe didn't like hospitals. She and her mommy had spent most of the day before there, smelling that awful smell and eating rubbery food and letting the doctor with the white coat poke on her and listen to her breathe in and out with that thing he hung around his neck.

She didn't know why he needed that thingamabob to hear her breathe. She could hear her own self breathe, and she could hear her mommy breathe without it.

But she was just five, and nobody listened to her except Mr. Mitch who finally brought her home after she'd begged and begged and poked her lips out. Mr. Mitch was a softie.

He didn't like to see her sad.

She giggled and snuggled into the covers, and tried to think about her daddy up in heaven and Mr. Mitch's wife up there, too. Todd said he was waiting to tell his daddy goodbye before he crossed through those shiny gates. He said his mama told him the gates were made of pearls and the streets made of gold.

Did they sparkle like the angel pin she bought her mommy?

Her mommy left the radio on, and she listened to the Christmas songs, *Jingle Bells* and *Rudolph the Red-nosed Reindeer* and *Santa Claus Is Coming to Town.*

Where was Santa Claus now?

She snuck out of bed and looked out the window, hunting for his reindeer and the sleigh in the sky. But she didn't see the sleigh, just the moon and lots of stars.

She picked out the shiny star the preacher talked about, the one that the Wise men followed so they could find the baby Jesus, and she closed her eyes and made a wish.

Maybe Santa could follow that star to find her.

She'd left him extra cookies and hoped he got the new picture she'd drawn. She wished she could spell and write out the words she wanted to say, but maybe he got lots of notes from kids and he'd understand her drawing. She wanted that kitty cat, but even more than that, she wanted to stay here and live on the ranch with her mommy and Mr. Mitch and Todd.

KAYLIE ROSE EARLY THE next morning, hoping CeCe would be happy with her presents. She had just poured herself a cup of coffee when a soft knock sounded at the back door.

She checked through the screen and saw Mitch. God, she'd missed him in bed last night. But CeCe had needed her after their horrendous day, and she had to start distancing herself from Mitch so it didn't hurt so much when she left.

Mitch wore a sheepish grin, his eyes hooded beneath that Stetson. "Santa left this outside."

Kaylie's heart pitched when she saw the tiny orange ball in his hands.

"Mitch?"

"I know I should have checked with you. Is it all right?"

"It's perfect," Kaylie said, then reached up and hugged him. "You've given CeCe everything she wanted this year."

When she pulled back, mixed emotions clouded his eyes, and she realized he was probably thinking about his son. Her heart ached for him.

Mitch moved past her, and they carried the kitten in the den. He built a fire while she put the turkey he'd bought the day before in the oven. Footsteps padded down the steps, then CeCe shrieked as she ran into the room and discovered the kitten.

"Santa brought him, Santa brought him!" CeCe squealed.

Kaylie laughed, her eyes watering as she looked up at Mitch. He was grinning, too, obviously pleased that he'd made CeCe so happy.

CeCe chased the kitten around, laughing and playing. "I'm gonna name her Orange," CeCe said as the kitten nuzzled her nose.

"Orange," Kaylie said with a laugh. "That's a good name."

"Can we open presents now?" CeCe asked.

Mitch ruffled CeCe's hair. "You don't want breakfast first?"

CeCe shook her head. "No, I'm too 'cited."

"Then let's open presents," Mitch agreed.

Kaylie handed CeCe the gifts she'd bought for her, and Mitch sipped coffee while she opened them.

"My cowboy boots and hat!" CeCe tugged on the boots and plopped the hat on her head then danced around. "Don't I look like a real cowboy now, Mr. Mitch?"

Mitch winked. "The prettiest cowgirl I've ever seen."

CeCe beamed with happiness at the paper dolls and jumped up and down with joy over the doll clothes, blanket, and bed Kaylie had made.

"Now it's your turn to open, Mommy." She ran to the tree and returned with two boxes.

One for her and one for Mitch.

CeCe bounced from one foot to the other, her eyes glittering. "Open it, Mommy."

Her daughter had been wrapping the present before Buckham had kidnapped them. But CeCe told her to hurry, and Kaylie banished the bad memories. They were safe now. Nothing was going to spoil their day.

She ran her finger over the glittering angel as she unwrapped the tissue. "I love it. It's beautiful, honey." She hugged CeCe then removed the pin and attached it to her sweater.

CeCe beamed, then handed Mitch a box wrapped in red paper. What in the world was in it? She hadn't helped CeCe pick out anything for him. They'd simply baked cookies.

Mitch's gaze met hers as he shook the box. "Hmm. I wonder what's in here. A tie maybe?"

Like he would wear a tie, Kaylie thought with a smile.

He tore open the paper, then lifted the lid of the shoebox. But his smile faded as he looked up at CeCe.

"Rocks?" Mitch asked in a gravelly voice.

Kaylie frowned, confused by his reaction and the gift. Then she remembered Mitch had taught CeCe how to skim stones the day they'd ridden to the pond.

CeCe rubbed the kitty's furry head. "Todd picked them out for you, Mr. Mitch. He wanted me to give them to you."

The color faded from Mitch's face, and he bolted up and strode outside.

Through the front door, she saw Mitch lean over the porch rail, his shoulders shaking.

CHAPTER 15

MITCH INHALED A PAIN-FILLED breath. How in the hell did CeCe know about the rocks?

Sure, he'd taught her to skip rocks that day at the pond, but he'd never mentioned how much Todd loved collecting the stones?

He'd boxed up Todd's collection and carried it to the cabin with him so there was no way CeCe had seen them.

The door squeaked open, Kaylie's sweet scent wafting toward him. "Mitch?"

"I'm sorry," he said in a thick voice. "That was real sweet of CeCe."

"She thinks you don't like them," Kaylie said.

He whirled around anger at the situation mingling with grief. "How could she know?"

"Know what?"

"That my son collected rocks? That it was a special thing we did together?"

Kaylie's face paled. "I don't know, Mitch."

"Does she always do stuff like that?"

"Like what?"

"Talk about . . . the dead like she can talk to them."

"No." Kaylie captured his hand in hers. He squeezed it, wanting to cling to her and her daughter. He felt guilty for having them here when his son and wife were dead.

But he didn't want them to leave either.

They'd filled his house with love, laughter, and happy memories, and given him something to live for.

"I don't understand, either," Kaylie said. "Maybe she saw a picture of Todd."

"There's no way, I boxed them up and stored them in the cabin."

Kaylie wet her lips. "Maybe she just senses him since she's staying in his room."

Footsteps clattered, and he looked down to see CeCe on the porch, the kitten cradled in her arms. "Todd says he loves you, Mr. Mitch. He's not mad at you, and he wants you to be happy again."

Mitch's breath stalled in his chest.

"He says not to be sad." CeCe sighed, her voice tentative. "That he's here with you."

A chill slithered down Mitch's neck yet at the same time, he felt a warmth on his hand. A warmth as if someone had touched him.

When he looked down though, there was nothing there.

Or was there?

Maybe in her childlike innocence, CeCe had connected with his son's spirit, and she was trying to relay a message. That his son didn't blame him. That he loved him.

That he'd always live in his heart.

Could he forgive himself?

Mitch glanced across the ranch, then at the *For Sale* sign dangling in the breeze. Yes, his son was here. He always would be.

There was no way he could sell the ranch and leave him.

THEY HAD A BEAUTIFUL Christmas Day. Kaylie cooked turkey and dressing with all the trimmings, and CeCe played with her kitten and paper dolls and wore her pink boots and cowboy hat all day.

Mitch seemed unusually quiet and left for a time that afternoon to visit his son's grave. When he returned, he seemed more relaxed, and the three of them shared dinner then rode out to the pond

But the morning after Christmas, Kaylie knew it was time for her and CeCe to leave. Mitch had made no attempt to kiss her again or make love to her. He hadn't mentioned wanting them to stay either.

He'd remained quiet all evening, almost somber as if he needed them to let him have his house to himself. Obviously, CeCe's comments about Todd had upset him.

She didn't understand her daughter either, but obviously, CeCe believed she'd connected with Mitch's little boy.

She rose early and packed her suitcase, then explained to CeCe that since the bad man was gone, they needed to return to their own house. She wanted to say goodbye to Mitch but was afraid that would be too hard on her daughter, so she left him a note and headed back to the house they'd left months ago.

"I don't wants to leave Horseshoe and the ranch," CeCe said with a pout. "Orange don't wanna go either."

"I know," Kaylie said, her chest aching. She wanted to stay, too. To make the ranch their permanent home. To be with Mitch.

But the ranch belonged to him, his son and his memories, and she had no right to intrude. He'd tolerated them because Buckham was trying to kill them, but now she had no reason to stay.

Except that she loved him.

But Mitch wasn't ready to hear that.

When she reached their old house, a sense of gloom swept over her. CeCe disappeared into a quiet funk, her eyes flaring with near panic as they neared the house.

"I don't wanna go in there," CeCe said.

Kaylie hesitated on the stoop and knelt to console her daughter. "I know we have bad memories here, but we had good ones, too."

CeCe shook her head, then started to cry. "No, I hate that house. I don't wanna live here anymore."

Kaylie looked up at the place she and Joe had bought together and remembered his lies.

Those lies had gotten him killed and nearly destroyed her and CeCe's lives.

She made a snap decision. They couldn't live here, not now, not ever again.

She would put the house on the market.

Then she and CeCe would find another house and start over.

———•———

THE MOMENT MITCH ENTERED the farmhouse, a sense of loneliness engulfed him.

The house was too quiet.

And Kaylie's car was gone. He told himself they might have just driven to town to run errands, but he spotted a note on the kitchen counter by the coffee machine, picked it up and read it, his heart in his throat.

> *Thank you for saving us, Mitch, and for giving us a wonderful Christmas. Your son was a lucky little boy to have you for a father. Don't forget that.*
>
> *Love, Kaylie & CeCe*

Mitch crushed the note in his fist. They were moving back to their own house.

He had saved their lives but lost them anyway.

Then he saw the small stones CeCe had given him. But they

weren't in the box as he'd left them. They were spread out on the table in the shape of a horseshoe.

Tears clogged his throat. Todd used to arrange the rocks in that same pattern.

He really was here . . .

Grief, anger, and need surged through him, and he strode through the house, missing Kaylie and CeCe. The Christmas tree was still standing, heavy with the ornaments they'd made.

But the lights weren't sparkling, and the presents were all gone as if yesterday had happened ages ago.

Todd's laughter, followed by CeCe's chatter, reverberated through the house. He could still smell the heavenly scent of apple pie and sugar cookies Kaylie and CeCe had baked. He could hear their laughter and feel the warmth they'd brought to his empty house and life.

He should have given Kaylie a present yesterday.

Maybe it wasn't too late. He could track them down and . . . do what? Take her something from the ranch to remember him by?

Did she want to remember him?

She'd admired the horse quilt she'd draped across CeCe's bed, and she had sewn placemats for the table. She hadn't needed expensive linens or fancy things.

She'd also liked the house and the antiques and . . . would she like his grandmother's antique ring?

And CeCe . . . she wanted Horseshoe. Would she have a horse to ride where she was going?

Suddenly unable to stand the idea of leaving the ranch or

living in the house without Kaylie and CeCe, he hurried up to the attic and dug inside his grandmother's velvet jewelry box. He found the antique silver ring with the rubies in it and jammed it in his pocket.

He wanted Kaylie to have it.

Hell, he wanted Kaylie and CeCe here on the ranch with him, too.

But even if she said no, he would give her the ring. She needed to know how much she meant to him.

That he'd been only a shell of a man before she'd walked into his life, a man drowning in booze and hurt.

A man who no longer cared about living anymore.

Until she'd given him a reason.

KAYLIE HAMMERED THE *FOR Sale* sign in the front yard while CeCe played with Orange in the grass. Neither of them had gone inside.

A cleaning crew had cleaned the bloodstains after the shooting, but she decided to let a friend she'd worked with handle the listing.

There was nothing she wanted in the house. The life she'd had with Joe had been a lie.

The sound of an engine roaring made her look up, and she spotted a truck barreling down the road.

Mitch's truck.

Her heart went pitter-patter.

CeCe squealed in excitement. "Mr. Mitch, Mr. Mitch!"

Mitch slowed the truck and parked on the curb. Kaylie tucked a strand of hair behind her ear and joined CeCe on the lawn. The truck door opened, and Mitch emerged, looking so handsome in his Stetson and jeans, that he robbed her breath.

Lord, she loved that sexy man. She'd only been away from him for hours, and she missed him so badly she wanted to run into his arms.

He strode toward them, his eyes sparkling in the morning light. "You left something behind."

Kaylie forced her voice to remain even. She couldn't throw herself at him when he obviously still loved his wife. "I'm sorry. I can go back and pack everything up."

Mitch's mouth twitched. "I wasn't talking about the tree or the decorations."

Kaylie frowned. "Then what?"

His eyes darkened. "You left *me* behind."

Hope budded inside Kaylie.

"I didn't wants to leave you," CeCe said, piping up.

A grin twitched at Mitch's mouth. "I didn't want you to leave, either, sweet pea."

Mitch dug in his pocket, spiking Kaylie's hopes even more. "I didn't give you your present yesterday."

She licked her lips. "You didn't have to get me anything."

"You liked my grandmother's antiques. I thought you might like this." He opened his palm to reveal a beautiful antique silver ring with glittering rubies.

"Mitch . . . I . . . it's gorgeous."

His gaze latched with hers. "You were wrong about me saving you, Kaylie. It was the other way around. You saved me."

"You were worth saving," she said, her throat thick with tears.

Mitch dropped to one knee. "I love you, and I love CeCe. Will you come back and live with me on the ranch?"

Kaylie stared at their joined hands, hardly able to believe her ears.

Happy tears filled Kaylie's eyes. "Oh, Mitch," Kaylie whispered. "I love you, too."

"Will you marry me?" Mitch asked gruffly.

Kaylie nodded. "Yes, of course, I'll marry you. I love you more than words."

Mitch kissed Kaylie's hand, then stood and pulled her in his arms and kissed her. CeCe threw herself at them as they pulled apart. "Santa did hear me!"

Mitch and Kaylie laughed, then he scooped CeCe and Orange into his arms and hugged them all to him.

"Can Horseshoe be my very own horsie, Mr. Mitch?"

Mitch kissed her cheek. "Yes, sweet pea. Horseshoe can be yours. I think Todd would like that."

Other Books

THE MANHUNT SERIES
Safe by His Side (Book 2)
Safe with Him (Book 3)

THE KEEPERS SERIES
Pretty Little Killers (Book 1)
Good Little Girls (Book 2)
Little White Lies (Prequel to Dead Little Darlings)
Dead Little Darlings (Book 3)

THE GRAVEYARD FALLS SERIES
All the Beautiful Brides (Book 1)
All the Pretty Faces (Book 2)
All the Dead Girls (Book 3)

THE SLAUGHTER CREEK SERIES
Before She Dies (Prequel)
Dying to Tell (Book 1)
Her Dying Breath (Book 2)
Worth Dying For (Book 3)
Dying for Love (Book 4)

THE DEMONBORN SERIES
Heartless (Book 1)
Mindless (Book 2)
Soulless (Book 3)

RITA'S LIGHTER SIDE
Marry Me, Maddie
Sleepless in Savannah
Love Me, Lucy
Husband Hunting 101
Here Comes the Bride
There Goes the Groom
Single and Searching
Under the Covers

ABOUT THE AUTHOR

USA TODAY AND AWARD-WINNING author Rita Herron fell in love with books at the ripe age of eight when she read her first Trixie Belden mystery. But she didn't think real people grew up to be writers, so she became a teacher instead. Now she writes so she doesn't have to get a real job!

With over ninety books to her credit, she's penned romantic suspense, romantic comedy, and YA stories, but she especially loves writing dark romantic suspense tales set in southern small towns.

For more on Rita and her titles, visit her at www.ritaherron.com. You can also follow her on Facebook and Twitter @ ritaherron.